HIS DR

M000309895

"This isn't go
about half a block bel.

Mika frowned. "Whachu talkin' 'bout?"

"Not enough cars on the street," he explained. "It's still dark out so I doubt that he can really make us out, but like I keep sayin', Mo's a paranoid sumbitch. Sooner or later, he gone notice a pair of headlights constantly in his rearview mirror."

"So kill the lights," Mika said.

"That's just an invitation for the cops to stop you, and do you really wanna get pulled over with what we got in this car?" Kane barked. "The coke. The guns. The keys and cell of some nigga shot dead in a motel room buck naked, with shit all over his dick?"

"Just do it," she ordered. "I'll handle the cops if it comes to that."

Kane looked unsure for a second, then did as suggested and turned his headlights off...

SHE'S HIS DRUG, HE'S HER THUG

His Drug, Her Thug Series
She's His Drug, He's Her Thug

SHE'S HIS DRUG, HE'S HER THUG

By

Nirvana Blaque

SHE'S HIS DRUG, HE'S HER THUG

If you purchased this book without a cover, you should be aware that this book is stolen property. It was reported as "unsold and destroyed" to the publisher, and neither the author nor the publisher has received any payment for this "stripped book."

This book is a work of fiction contrived by the author, and is not meant to reflect any actual or specific person, place, action, incident or event. Any resemblance to incidents, events, actions, locales or persons, living or dead, factual or fictional, is entirely coincidental.

Copyright © 2020 by Nirvana Blaque.

This book is published by Fat Boy Publishing.

All rights reserved, including the right to reproduce this book or portions thereof in any form whatsoever. For information, address Fat Boy Publishing, P.O. Box 2727, Cypress, TX 77410.

ISBN: 978-1-937666-52-1

Printed in the U.S.A.

SHE'S HIS DRUG, HE'S HER THUG

ACKNOWLEDGMENTS

I would like to thank the following for their help with this book: GOD first and foremost, for continuing to shower me with blessings, and my family, for all their love and support.

SHE'S HIS DRUG, HE'S HER THUG

Thank you for purchasing this book! If you enjoyed it, please feel free to leave a review on the site from which it was purchased.

Also, if you would like to be notified when I release new books, please subscribe to my mailing list via the following link: http://eepurl.com/gShzML

Finally, for those who may be interested, I have included my blog and social media info:

Blog: https://nirvanablaque.blogspot.com/

Facebook: https://www.facebook.com/nirvana.black.3597

Twitter: https://twitter.com/BlaqueNirvana

PROLOGUE

Mika moaned as Tweet lay on top of her, his face buried in her neck, thrusting between her legs, going deep inside her. The moan was legit – that shit felt good – but he wasn't getting her there.

Come on, nigga, *she thought.* Work that dick!

Most times, Tweet had no trouble getting her off. They weren't a couple (fuck, they weren't even dating, *just fooling around every now and then), but he knew how to throw down in the sheets. Plus, she hadn't had any dick in weeks! Making her cum should have been as easy pissing on the floor (which most niggas have a fuckin' degree in).*

Horny as she was, she knew the problem wasn't her. It was him. *He wasn't slangin' that dick like he normally did – rhythm and shit was all off. Muthafucka was distracted or something. She didn't know where his head was.*

Well, I know where a *certain* head is, *she thought, giggling.*

Tweet stopped mid-thrust, raising up and looking at her.

"What da fuck is funny?" he asked.

"Nuthin'," Mika said, not wanting to deal with a muthafuckin' ego trip when all she wanted was some deep dickin'. Oh well, sometimes a bitch gotta take over. "Let me on top."

A few seconds later she was straddling him, holding his rock-hard dick upright and groaning audibly as she slid down over it.

Oh yeah, *she thought as she started rocking her hips.* Now this shit is on…

****

Mika took her time in the shower, trying to figure out if she was going to stay over. Unlike a lot of niggas, Tweet was cool if a bitch wanted to spend the night; he didn't magically transform into a

1

muthafuckin' asshole after getting his dick wet. That's why she didn't mind breaking him off a piece whenever he asked her out. (It also didn't hurt that he was decent – didn't act like a bitch had to go down on him just because he bought yo ass a cold burger on a stale bun, with a side of soggy-ass fries.)

Of course, this thing between them was just casual – something that happened every month or two, when one of them had an itch that needed to be scratched. He'd take her out to eat or maybe a movie, and then they'd end up back at his place, dick and pussy slamming together like a pair of fuckin' magnets. (Although tonight, they hadn't gone out. Mika had just been horny as fuck and made a booty call, and Tweet had told her to bring her sweet ass on over.)

She turned off the shower, stepped out and grabbed a nearby bath towel. A minute later she was clean, fresh and dry. Using the towel, she wiped off the steamed-up mirror and took a good look at herself.

At five-eight, she was a nice height, with hair cut in a short bob that neatly framed an angelic, mocha-brown face. Her perfect hourglass figure was made up of tits that were like cantaloupes and firm as shit (which is what you expect at nineteen), a slim waist with provocative hips, and an ass that looked like it was sculpted by an artist.

Bitch, you fine as fuck, *she said to herself, smiling.* If you could can that shit and sell it, you'd be rich!

Still grinning, she stepped out of the bathroom and back into the bedroom, where she had expected to find Tweet fast asleep. The bed was empty, though.

Mika frowned. Normally, when she put the pussy on a muthafucka like she'd done Tweet – damn near ridin' his ass into the sunset – a nigga would wanna sleep for days. As a matter of fact–

Her train of thought was cut off as a muted popping noise and a flash of light made her jump. Looking towards the window, she saw and heard fireworks going off. She relaxed slightly, remembering that it was the Fourth of July. (In fact, while she had been gliding up and down Tweet's pole, some kind of rocket had gone off, filling the sky outside with glittering white sparks just as she came, like some symbolic shit you'd see in a movie.)

Now that she thought about it, maybe the fireworks had woken Tweet up. (Or some nigga firing a gun, which was the local version of fireworks in some parts of the hood.) He probably just went to the kitchen for a drink of water or something.

Still naked, she headed for the bedroom door and was about to open it when she heard voices coming from the other side. Sounded like they were arguing, too.

Dammit, Tweet, *she thought angrily.* If that's your fuckin' girlfriend…

She let the thought trail off. She wasn't mad at the notion of Tweet having a girlfriend – hadn't even cared enough to ask. (And if the bitch was taking care of her man, he wouldn't be calling her *on the regular, begging to lick her coochie and shit…) No, Mika was upset that the muthafucka might have pulled her into some drama, because* that *she didn't need.*

Warily, she cracked open the door and peeked out into the living room. She let out a sigh of relief when she realized that it wasn't a girl Tweet was talking to; it was just some nigga – two of 'em, in fact. Tweet, dressed in nothing but pajama bottoms, was sitting on the sofa, while one of the guys – some wannabe gangsta by the look of him – stood in front of him, a few feet away. The other guy stood by the door.

"Look," Tweet was saying, "I know I fucked up, but I'll fix it. I will. I promise I will."

Listening to him, Mika suddenly realized that Tweet was nervous as fuck. And just as quickly, she realized she might have wandered into a situation that was a lot more serious than some jealous bitch.

SHE'S HIS DRUG, HE'S HER THUG

Tweet wasn't rich, but he always had money. He also had a nice ride and a decent apartment. For a nigga with practically no education and no real job, that only meant one thing: he was doing shady shit to get by.

Now, there's lots of shit niggas can do on the dee-el in order to make money on the street, and not all of it's crazy dangerous. Muthafuckas can shoplift, fence shit, pimp bitches out... Mika always thought Tweet was doing something along those lines, but from the conversation in the next room it was sounding like he'd gotten into some serious shit.

"How you gonna fix shit, huh?" asked the guy in front of Tweet. "Muthafucka, this ain't just about replacing what you took, it's about the message. We let yo ass slide, and every nigga on the street think they can fuck us with an elephant dick."

"Naw, Jaycee," Tweet pleaded. "It won't even be like that. Nobody'll know—"

There was a sound like a cannon going off, cutting Tweet off. At the same time, his body seemed to jerk wildly, with his shoulders flying forward for a second, like someone had hit him in the chest with a sledgehammer. A moment later, his shoulders went back to their normal position while his arms flopped down uselessly at his sides. His head seemed to teeter from side to side for a second, then fell back as blood started pouring from a hole on the left side of his chest.

"Fuck, Jay!" yelled the guy by the door. "You didn't give him chance to tell us where the shit was!"

Jaycee, holding a small handgun, looked unconcerned. "I was tired of listenin' to his bullshit, Kane. Besides, it's gotta be here somewhere."

Mika, who had involuntarily jumped at the sound of the gunshot (and then covered her mouth to keep from screaming) remained glued to the door, almost in shock.

4

SHE'S HIS DRUG, HE'S HER THUG

Kane shook his head in disbelief. "Well, you put us on the clock when you shot 'im – sounded like a muhfuckin' bomb went off in here. Cops probably on they way."

"Just chill, man," Jaycee shot back. "It's the Fourth. Niggas gonna be shootin' guns and shit all night 'round here."

"Not in the building, shithead," Kane insisted.

"Will you stop bitchin' and just look for our shit?" Jaycee asked as he tucked the gun in a pocket of the hoodie he was wearing. "I'll check the kitchen and out here; you scope out the bedroom."

Mika, who had been frozen until then, suddenly realized that she was fucked. Unlike the movies, there was no fire escape or any shit like that to slip out of and get away.

Her first instinct was to revert to childhood form and hide under the bed. But if they were trying to find something, that was the first place these assholes would look. That left the bathroom and Tweet's closet, which was the reach-in type, with two sets of bi-fold, shutter-like doors.

All of this flashed through her head in a second, and she was in motion almost before she had consciously made the decision: the closet. It was closer – right next to the bedroom door – it only took her a moment to quietly slip inside. She closed the door just in time, as Kane (whom she could see through the shutters on the door) entered the bedroom.

Later, Mika would reflect on the fact that he was tall – probably six-two – handsome, and well-built. There was a kind swagger to the way he walked, an easy confidence, as if he was in control of everything in his environment. Under other circumstances, he was the kind of nigga she would drop her panties for in a heartbeat.

At the moment, however, she was terrified and couldn't stop shaking. Wanting to put as much distance as possible between them, she quietly slid to the back of the closet, slipping behind what appeared to be some winter coats and jogging suits that were hanging up, never taking her eyes off Kane.

5

SHE'S HIS DRUG, HE'S HER THUG

On his part, Kane seemed to take in the room at a glance, mentally noting everything in sight: the dresser, bed, bathroom, window, and so on. As predicted, his first course of action was to look under the bed (although he pulled out a pair of gloves and put them on first). However, he didn't get down on all fours like she thought he would and peek under there. Instead, he simply bent down, gripped the underside of the mattress with one hand (with Mika noting that he held a gun in the other), and then lifted the whole thing.

Pillows and blankets went sliding to the floor with barely audible hisses. Kane ignored them as he seemingly inspected the items under the bed. Mika couldn't see them clearly, but got the impression that there were some hand weights, a few small boxes, and some other things she couldn't quite make out.

Using his foot, Kane slid a couple of items from under the bed and then let the mattress drop back down. Mika noted that the items appeared to be shoe boxes, which Kane – still using only his feet – tilted over one by one. They all seemed to contain nothing but sneakers. Expensive ones, endorsed by the latest NBA superstar, but shoes nonetheless.

Frowning, Kane surveyed the room again, then walked over to the closet. He studied the two sets of doors for a moment, then seemed to mentally flip a coin. Mika let out a soft sigh of relief as he opened the doors at the other end of her hiding place. However, she was a long way from being home free. Assuming he didn't find what he was looking for there, he was clearly headed for her side of the closet next.

Light from the bedroom spilled into the closet around him, giving her a solid view of his profile from her position. He looked the place up and down, then began spreading the hanging items apart so that he could thoroughly search the area. After a minute or two (which seemed like forever to Mika), he finally closed the closet door.

Mika had never been much for prayer, but she closed her eyes now and prayed to heaven for a miracle.

"Got it" Jaycee shouted from the living room.

Not believing her luck, Mika warily opened her eyes and almost gasped at how close she'd come to getting caught: Kane's hand was on the knob of the closet.

"Where?" Kane yelled back.

"Pantry," Jaycee answered. "Unoriginal muhfucka..."

Kane let out a slight chuckle and took his hand off the knob. Mika almost wanted to shout "Hallelujah!" as he turned and began walking towards the door. However, her joy was short-lived.

Just as he reached the threshold, Kane stopped. He then turned back towards the interior of the bedroom, an intense frown on his face. One look at him, and Mika knew that she was busted.

No, No, NO!!! *she thought, almost in a panic.* Just leave, nigga!

But the nigga didn't leave. Somehow, he knew that something was off, and she realized what it was a moment later when Kane, brow still crinkled, headed towards Tweet's dresser. And there it was: her purse.

Mika wanted to fuckin' scream. She had left her purse on the dresser, as she normally did when they came back here. Usually, when she got back home (whether the same night or the next morning), she'd find that Tweet had slipped her a little something – usually a couple of twenties.

It wasn't trickin'. She never, ever promised Tweet pussy and he never offered to pay. It was just something he had started doing as a nice gesture. If she'd asked him for cash and not given him a taste, she knew that he would still have given her the money. Likewise, if he didn't put anything in her purse, she wouldn't be upset.

Regardless, the purse was a fuckin' red flag, and a second after picking it up Kane was rifling through it. Abruptly, he set the purse back down and scanned the floor; in almost no time at all, he found her clothes under the blankets and shit that had slid off the bed. A moment later, he was off – headed to the bathroom. Naturally it

7

wouldn't take long to check the tub and toilet, maybe under the cabinets if he thought a woman was desperate (or small) enough. As she suspected, he was out of there in about ten seconds, maybe less.

Watching his eyes sweep the room, Mika knew he'd realize there was only one place left to look. As if reading her mind, he stepped to the closet door where she was hiding and yanked it open. He then immediately reached out and spread apart the clothes hanging on the rack in front of her.

Their eyes locked, and even though she was standing there in all her glory, he kept his eyes on her face. Mika was scared shitless and it showed. He was still holding the gun, but she was too fucking scared to even beg for her life. Instead, she just stood there, speechless, waiting for him to bust a cap in her ass.

Kane just stared for a moment, then he glanced at something he was holding in his free hand. With a shock, she realized it was her driver's license.

"Da fuck you doing in there – takin' a nap?" Jaycee shouted from the other room.

"Fuck you," Kane replied casually, still looking at Mika. "Tweet had some sneakers back here I was thinkin' of takin', but it's too much fuckin' trouble. Five-oh can track all kinds of shit these days."

"True dat," Jaycee said. "So leave that shit and let's fuckin' roll."

"A'ight," Kane stated. He held up Mika's license so she could clearly see it, then turned and headed towards the door. "Let's send the boys back to torch this muhfucka – don't wanna leave any DNA."

"Good idea," Jaycee agreed.

"Shouldn't take 'em more than twenty minutes to get here after we clear out," Kane said, speaking more over his shoulder than to Jaycee, who grumbled something in reply that Mika didn't catch. A few seconds later, she heard the door open and close, and for the

first time in what seemed like forever, she felt like she could breathe again.

She stumbled out of the closet, shaking like someone had shoved a snow cone up her snatch. For a moment, she felt like she was going to throw up, but something in the back of her mind screamed, "Bitch, move yo ass!"

She listened to the voice. Kane had given her a heads-up: she had about twenty minutes to clear the fuck out before Tweet's place turned into a barbeque joint. Shee-it, she'd be ghost long before that. Matter of fact, it was all she could do not to run out the muthafcukin' door buck naked, but she held it together long enough to get her clothes on and make sure she had all her shit.

She spent a moment at the door, peeking out the peephole to make sure nobody was around. Not that it mattered; wouldn't take much to figure out she was one of the last people to see Tweet alive. (Not to mention her DNA was all over his dick, his fingers, his lips…)

She spared a glance back at Tweet. He looked fucked up, but death will do that to a nigga. She didn't know what he'd been involved in, but the asshole had almost gotten her killed. (And still might, since that nigga Kane now knew where she lived thanks to her license.)

Can't go home, *she realized.* But I gotta get the fuck up up outta here.

Mind made up, she slipped out the door, damn near ran all the way down to the bottom floor, and jetted out into the night…

SHE'S HIS DRUG, HE'S HER THUG

Chapter 1

The night Tweet died, Mika had been too scared to go home. She'd basically scraped together what cash she could and gotten on the first bus out of town. (She'd told her family some bullshit about an old boyfriend showing up and taking her on a trip.)

After that, it had been five months of basically roaming from town to town. She had a few skills she knew how to put to use: shoplifting, pole-dancing, and Three-Card Monte, to name a few. (That last came courtesy of an ex-boyfriend, who taught her how to run the con by having her act as his shill.) They were all talents she could use to hustle – to earn a few bucks wherever she went. It was generally enough to keep her fed and off the streets, but – even with soup kitchens and homeless shelters – it was a fucking hand-to-mouth existence, and there were a couple of stretches where she had to go days literally living off a loaf of bread and water. The last month or so had been fuckin' brutal, though.

First of all, with the weather changing (it started getting cold as a bitch around October), it had gotten hard to get niggas to hang around on street corners to play card games and shit. Plus – depending on where she set up – she occasionally had muthafuckas rollin' up saying that she was operating on *their* corners and demanding a cut. Depending on how business was going (and whether it seemed like the niggas confrontin' her were full of shit), sometimes she paid, sometimes she didn't, and sometimes she just moved to a different spot.

On top of that, when November and the holiday season rolled around, stores started hiring extra security and were watching muthafuckas like a hawk every time you set foot inside. She was actually on the verge of stealing some shit in a department store when some nigga grabbed a necklace off a nearby jewelry counter and went streakin' towards the exit. A security guard hit his ass with a blindside tackle right before he got to the door and sent him flying into a display of snowglobes that were on sale. Muthafucka ended up laying on the floor moaning and shit, all wet and covered with broken glass as the other guards showed up. In fact, he was screaming about a piece of glass being in his eye when they dragged his ass away in cuffs. But the real kicker was that one of the security folks that took his as away was some bitch in plainclothes, and she'd been standing not five feet away when Mika was about to lift some shit. Counting herself lucky, she got the fuck out of there and took shoplifting off her résumé.

It was then, with her sources of income drying up, that she realized she was running out of options. Pretty soon, she'd have to either go back home or start trickin'.

Now, Mika had done a lot of shit in her day that she wasn't proud of – you had to when you left home at sixteen: fucked a guy on the first date (even in the hood bitches tried not to do that shit, but some niggas just got game); stole money out the offering tray at church; gone down on a woman; sold a little weed on the side to make ends meet. She even took it up the ass from some nigga she thought was special. (He wasn't.) But she had never turned tricks.

The final fuckin' straw, however, the thing that made the decision for her, was when two niggas pulled her ass into a dark alley one night when she was on her way home from a soup kitchen. One moment she was just struttin' along, trying to figure out what her next move was gonna be, and the next some muthafucka was slappin' his hand over her mouth and wrappin' his other arm around her torso while another nigga grabbed her ankles. In two seconds, they had her in the alley, and it seemed like nobody on the street had seen a muthafuckin' thing (and there had been a decent number of niggas out there). Or if they had seen anything, they didn't care enough to scream "Let that lady go!" or any shit like that.

Fortunately, Mika had the benefit of not just growing up in the hood, but also with five siblings, including three older brothers. Basically, she knew how to fight niggas.

She managed to wrench one leg free and then kicked out at the face of the nigga holding her ankles, her heel connecting solidly with his nose and lips. At the same time, she drew her lips back as much as possible and bit down hard on one of the fingers over her mouth, trying to make her teeth meet.

The nigga holding her legs yelped and dropped her feet, his hands going to his face. The one covering her mouth screeched as he ripped his hand away, also letting her go. As a result, she dropped unceremoniously to the ground, letting out a soft groan of pain as she banged her head on the concrete of the alley.

It being late November (just after Thanksgiving, in fact), the ground wasn't just hard, but fuckin' cold and wet, too, from melting snow and ice. Thankfully, the fake leather jacket she was wearing kept her back dry, but the ass of the jeans she was wearing got soaked immediately, as did the spot where her head had hit the ground.

The nigga who'd had her legs was bent over, still holding his face. (It was dark, but it looked like blood was running through his fingers. Mika drew in her leg and kicked out hard again, this time at the muthafucka's shin.

12

He yelped and reached for the injured leg, hopping on one foot for a second before he hit a patch of ice and ended up on his ass.

Feeling something foreign in her mouth, Mika spat it out as she rolled over and drew her legs up under her. Coming to her feet, she now faced the nigga who'd had his hand over her mouth. (Later, she'd realize that what she'd spat out was the fleshy part of one of his fingers.)

"Fuckin' bitch," he hissed, cradling the hand she'd bitten. "We were just gonna tear that pussy up, but now… Now, when we done, I'm gonna smash a muhfuckin' beer bottle and shove that shit up in you."

He rushed her then, arms outstretched, reaching for her throat. Mika flicked her right arm in an arc in front of her, and that nigga yanked his hands back, screaming like a slave being branded on his nutsack. Now he held both his hands loosely in front of him, trying to figure out what the fuck had happened.

Mika smiled to herself. While that nigga had been talking about all the shit he was gonna do to her pussy, she had quickly reached into her jacket pocket and pulled out Pierce – her switchblade. Pierce was like her fuckin' Siamese twin: she never went anywhere without him. That muthafucka had been so busy thinking 'bout ways to mutilate her twat that he hadn't even heard the blade spring open. But he sure as shit felt it when Pierce cut across his fuckin' hands. Now he stood there, lip trembling, snot starting to run down his nose as Mika advanced on him.

She swung Pierce and he instinctively put his hands out, screaming as he took defensive cuts on his palms and fingers. She brought the blade back the other way, missing this time as the nigga scrambled backwards for a second before tripping over his own feet. He tried get back up, but howled in pain after reflexively putting his hands on the ground for balance and trying to use them to rise; they couldn't take the weight. He ended up on his knees as Mika came after him like a fuckin' mad dog, damn near foaming at the mouth.

She sliced at him two more times in quick succession (going for his face, in all honesty, but again getting his hands as he put them out protectively). At that juncture, some intuition apparently told him to change tactics or he'd have no fuckin' fingers. Tucking his hands in towards his midsection, he rolled himself into a tight, whimpering ball, leaving his back and head exposed. She got in a couple of swipes at the muthafucka's head, giving him a wicked-ass part down the middle of his scalp and opening up a line along his forehead that ran temple-to-temple.

She was so enraged, so caught up in fury, that she might have continued slicing at that nigga indefinitely, but suddenly a pair of arms closed around her, lifting her off the ground and pulling her away.

"Gotcha, you bitch!" someone yelled near her ear.

Shit! She thought. She'd gotten so caught up in punishing the one muthafucka that she'd forgotten about his fuckin' partner-in-crime.

He had her in a bear hug from behind; her upper arms were, for the most part, pinned to her sides, but her forearms (and more importantly, her hands) were still free and had some range of motion.

Using Pierce, she jabbed behind her right leg, three times in quick succession, meeting resistance each time, like she was sticking a butcher knife into a slab of roast beef. The nigga holding her screamed and let her go.

Managing to stay on her feet, she spun around, Pierce still in her hand, ready to go on the attack.

The muthafucka who'd put her in the bear hug flopped down on his ass, holding his right side. Even in the dimness of the alley she could see he was bleeding, although she couldn't make out whether she'd stabbed him in the midsection, hip, or somewhere else. (Not that it fuckin' mattered; whatever he got, he deserved worse.)

Somewhat in control of her senses now, she dashed out of the alley and headed home.

****

"Home" at the time was a five-by-ten foot storage unit with twenty-four-hour access. Living in those places was illegal as fuck, but if you pecked around you could usually find a manager or owner willing to look the other way – especially if you slipped him something extra under the table. (It was also *waaay* fuckin' cheaper than just about anything else out there, gave you a safe place to stash your shit, and could be halfway comfortable if it was climate controlled like hers was.)

The storage facility was actually fenced, and she had to enter a code to get through the gate and onto the grounds. Once there, she headed straight to the ladies room to wash up. It wasn't until the door to the restroom actually closed behind her that she felt herself relax a little, and at that point she realized two things.

First, she'd never put Pierce away, and had instead walked the mile-and-a-half from the alley with the switchblade still open, dripping blood. However, she didn't worry too much about anything being traced back to her; those two assholes in the alley, despite being mutilated and maimed, were unlikely to tell anybody what really happened. Plus, with shit snowing, freezing over, and then melting almost every damn day, there wouldn't much of a trail to follow – even if anybody was so inclined. (Also, even though she hadn't been paying close attention – she didn't think Pierce had dripped *all* the way home.)

The second thing she realized was that she had left her purse; it had fallen off her while she was fightin' those two niggas in the alley. The good news was that the purse (which was a fake designer bag), was just a decoy. Since going on the run, she always carried anything worthwhile on her person – usually stuffed down her bra: cash, keys, cell phone (although that occasionally went into her back pocket), etcetera. However, a woman walking around without a purse – especially when shopping – stands out like a nigga at a Klan rally, so she typically carried one around just for show. It was basically just full of tissue paper and shit like that, but made her look less suspicious when she was trying to lift shit (and gave her a place to put it).

Long story short, she didn't worry about the purse. Sure, her prints were on it, but she'd never been arrested so she wasn't in the system. Even if she was and the purse got found next to a couple of knifed, would-be rapists, she could always just say she got mugged.

Putting the purse out of her mind, she stepped to one of the two sinks in the restroom and, after turning the water on, rinsed out her mouth. After she was certain the taste of blood was gone (and wishing that she'd bitten that nigga's finger off for covering her mouth), she began rinsing Pierce off. Once she was satisfied it was clean, she grabbed a couple of paper towels and thoroughly – damn near lovingly – dried the switchblade before folding it and putting it into her back pocket. (It had come in so handy tonight that she actually wanted to kiss the fuckin' thing.)

Next, she took off her jacket and inspected it. It was black faux leather – not particularly thick, but it kept the cold out. Holding it in a particular way under the light, she thought she could see stains in certain areas (such as the cuffs and at the bottom), but she wet some paper towels, dabbed soap on them from the bathroom dispenser, and was just starting to scrub at the jacket when a flush sounded in one of the stalls.

Mika froze. She hadn't even thought to check any of the four stalls when she came in. She wasn't the only person using a storage facility as a residence – there were whole fuckin' families living in some units – and she suddenly realized someone may have seen her cleaning blood off a blade and a jacket. She could come up with a plausible explanation, but on the surface the shit just didn't look good.

She let out a sigh of relief as the last stall opened and a little girl, maybe eight years old, came out. She was cute as button, with her hair in pigtails and wearing a dress. The girl's family might be going through tough times, but they were obviously still focusing on the little things like appearance and grooming.

The girl simply stared at her for a moment, obviously wary of strangers. Mika gave her what she felt was a friendly smile and the girl smiled back before going to the sink to wash her hands. That said, she watched Mika studiously in the mirror, eyeing her almost like a cop.

A moment later, the girl finished up and took a couple of paper towels. Drying her hands as she walked towards the door, she suddenly turned back towards Mika.

"You have blood on your pants," the little girl said, indicating Mika's right side.

Mika did a half-turn, checking herself out in the mirror. As the little girl had pointed out, there was blood on her pants near the side and back of the thigh area. It wasn't enough to make you think someone had been murdered, but it was a hell of a lot more than you'd get from a paper cut.

Trying to come up with something to say, Mika floundered for a moment before finally stating, "I know. I slipped and cut my leg on some broken glass."

The little girl seemed to consider this, then frowned. "So why aren't your jeans cut?"

Rather than wait for Mika to respond, the little girl just turned and left with a don't-bullshit-a-bullshitter look on her face.

Deciding that she didn't need any more unsolicited commentary from prepubescents, Mika tied her jacket around her waist to hide anything else on her pants, then grabbed the rest of paper towels and headed to her unit.

The door to her storage space was a roll-up model, secured by a padlock. Taking the key from her bra, she removed the padlock, opened the door and quickly stepped inside. She rolled the door back down, and then spent a moment eyeing her residence.

At five feet wide and ten feet deep, it was about half the size of a decent bedroom. That said, the place had obviously been used as a residence before, as evidenced by the fact that, when Mika moved in, there was already a line strung across the back of the unit for hanging wet clothes on. (In fact, she had the towel she'd used to wash up with that morning hanging up there now.) Someone had also installed a lock hasp and staple on the interior, so the unit could be padlocked from the inside, which Mika now did. There was always a chance that some fuckface would come along and put a lock on the outside while she was in here, but then she could always just claim that she was checking on her possessions when some asshole locked her inside.

Her meager belongings were pretty much all contained in three items: a backpack that held toiletries for the most part; a large duffel bag that contained the bulk of her clothes and which doubled as a pillow; and a wheeled carryon that housed a couple of blankets, as well as an assortment of odds and ends (like playing cards).

Mika stripped off everything she was wearing except for her panties and bra and inspected them. Other than the jeans, the only piece of clothing with blood on it was a long-sleeved t-shirt she'd been sporting.

Throwing on some sweats that also served as pajamas, she took the t-shirt and jeans back to the ladies room and washed out the blood in the sink. Then she hustled back to her unit and hung the wet clothes on the line at the back. (Although a couple of people saw her going to and from the restroom, washing apparel wasn't unusual here so she hadn't done anything to rouse suspicion.)

Having accomplished all she could for the moment, Mika finally took a breather by throwing a blanket on the floor (which could get cold at night despite being a climate-controlled unit) and turned her mind back to the problem at hand as she pulled another blanket on top of her.

After that shit in the alley, she felt like she was done. Being on the run seemed just as likely to kill her as that nigga who had taken her driver's license. Maybe it was time to call an end to this shit.

SHE'S HIS DRUG, HE'S HER THUG

She took her cell phone out of her bra, then followed up by taking out the cash, keys and all that other shit, until her tits no longer had any roommates. It seemed amazing to her that she could walk around the whole damn day with all that shit shoved in next to her girls. When she had first started carrying stuff that way (shortly after the third time a muthafucka had tried to steal her purse), it had been uncomfortable as hell. Now, she barely noticed. (Hell, half the time she fell asleep will all that shit still in place.)

She spent a moment looking at the phone. It was one of the few perks she'd kept after taking off like a bat outta hell. It was in her grandmomma's name, so it wasn't a direct link to her. (Assuming anybody was inclined to look for shit like that.) Still, she typically only used it to call home every few weeks – usually when she was about to leave one city for another – so if somebody was trying to use her cell to figure out where she was, they'd only know where she'd been, not where she was going. Plus, that was detective-type shit; she'd never known niggas in the hood to use technology and shit to track anybody down.

The only other thing she'd used the phone for was to check the obituaries in her hometown, and a few days after she left, she saw what she'd been expecting: an obit for Anthony "Tweet" Robin. However, rather than say anything about a fire, it said he'd been killed in a home invasion. (Not that how he died mattered. Dead was dead – end of fuckin' story.)

The real question, though, was whether she'd risk dying to go home, or keep going as she was now: living in fucking storage units, eating at soup kitchens, risking getting raped (and maybe murdered) in cold, dark alleys.

Fuck it, she finally said to herself and started dialing.

SHE'S HIS DRUG, HE'S HER THUG

Chapter 2

Mika never thought she would miss the city. She'd always felt that if she could just get away – go somewhere and start over – she'd put the thought of this limp-dick town out of her mind forever.

Well, she'd gotten away, alright. But she had pretty much left without anything: almost no cash, few resources...not even a fuckin' plan. Looking back, she suddenly realized that – after what happened to Tweet – she had essentially run like one of them dumb white bitches in a horror movie, who do all kinds of stupid shit when a killer's after them, such as hidin' in a closet. (Well actually, she *had* hid in a closet, and that shit hadn't worked out any better for her than it did for those snowflakes in the movies.) The bottom line, however, was that Mika had gotten the fuck outta Dodge. But now, five months later, she was back.

She'd made a couple of phone calls from her storage unit the night she was attacked, finally working on getting the answers she needed. All of her previous calls home had basically been short – mostly just efforts to let her family know she was okay. (She hadn't needed or wanted anybody thinking she was missing and trying to find her.) However, she had never asked any pointed questions because, first off, that shit would have looked suspicious as a muthafucka: *Yeah, I know I just left town all of a sudden, but it was totally legit – nothing shady. But on a side note, has anybody been looking for me?* Second, she'd always figured that if someone was making noise trying to find her, people would tell her about it without her asking – even on calls that only lasted a few minutes.

21

SHE'S HIS DRUG, HE'S HER THUG

This time, although she'd still beaten around the bush and not asked anything directly, she'd put some effort into getting the information she wanted. What she found out caused a weight she wasn't even aware of to suddenly lift off her shoulders.

First and foremost, nobody had been looking for her since she left. Nobody new, that is. Old boyfriends and shit had occasionally asked family and friends about her (and her boss at the fast-food place where she'd worked had wondered where the fuck she'd run off to), but nothing sinister. No collection agencies calling to talk about how fucked up her credit would be if she didn't take care of certain bills. No detectives wanting to ask her a few questions about a homicide. But mostly, no armed gangsta muthafuckas trying to figure out where she was.

With that issue settled, it had then just become a matter of finding a place to stay for a bit until she got back on her feet. When she left, she'd been living in a little efficiency apartment on a month-to-month lease. She wasn't quite ready to go back to that; she didn't have the funds for a security deposit and was still nervous about getting shit in her own name. Fortunately, her cousin Nay-Nay took care of living arrangements for her in a fuckin' heartbeat. (Actually, it was Nay-Nay's man Willie who set something up for her. Frankly speaking, Mika didn't really like Willie and didn't want any favors from him, but beggars can't be choosers.)

Basically, before she closed her eyes in the storage unit that last night, shit was already in place for Mika to come back home. The next morning, she'd washed up in the restroom, packed all her shit and then made a beeline for the bus station, buying the first available ticket home.

SHE'S HIS DRUG, HE'S HER THUG

And now that she was back, she realized how much she had missed the place. The sights, the sounds…everything. It was amazing (and bizarre) how some stuff could just trigger nostalgia: Niggas trying to sell stolen shit on street corners. Burned-out cars sitting on neglected, overgrown lots. Even the smell of piss wafting from an alleyway. Each of them, in a weird way, made her feel like (and aware of the fact that) she was home.

****

The first order of business, of course, was getting set up in the place that her cousin had found for her. Nay-Nay, who picked her up at the bus station, drove her straight there. It turned out to be a furnished one bedroom with one bath, located in the projects – specifically, the ninth floor of a high-rise in the middle of the hood.

Mika couldn't say she was surprised; no way was anybody gonna give her a penthouse apartment or some shit like that. And, as she'd known, the place came with strings attached.

"Look," Nay-Nay told her when they got there, "it ain't fancy but it's free, and there's only one thing you gotta do to stay here."

"Okay, what?" Mika asked, hoping this wasn't some type of prostitute gig. She'd told Nay-Nay she wasn't down for that shit, but sometimes the bitch didn't listen.

"It ain't nuthin' crazy," Nay-Nay assured her. "Basically, there's this package in the cabinet over the fridge in the kitchen. Sometime in the next week, you gone get a call. It's just gone give you a date and a time, like 'Tomorrow, noon,' 'Wednesday, three o'clock,' or some shit like that. Now, there's a vent in the hallway outside across from the door, down by the floor next to the stairwell. When the date and time come, you just take the package and put it in the vent – the cover just pops off and on."

They were currently in the living room of what would be Mika's new home, with Mika seated in an old recliner and her cousin across from her on a sofa. A quick tour had revealed that the furniture and appliances (almost everything, in fact) was cheap and dated, but the place was clean – or as clean as you could expect in the projects. According to Nay-Nay, there were even fresh sheets on the bed. (Ordinarily, Mika wouldn't have believed any shit like that, but she trusted her cousin.)

At the moment, Mika was still listening, thinking there would be more, but Nay-Nay didn't say anything else.

"So that's it?" Mika finally asked. "That's all I gotta do to stay here?"

"Well, a new package will show up about once a week," Nay-Nay said, "but it's the same routine every time: you'll get a call, put it in the vent, fuckin' rinse and repeat."

"What if I'm not here to answer the phone?"

"There's a machine. Check that bitch on the regular."

"What about the person calling?"

Nay-Nay frowned. "What about 'em?"

"They not worried 'bout leaving a message on an answerin' machine?"

"They'll be calling from a burner, but don't get cute and try to star-sixty-nine them or anything. That shit won't go over well."

"Well, what if somebody sees me puttin' shit in the vent?"

"Are you fuckin' braindead? It's gonna take like two seconds to do this shit. Fuckin' crackheads can find a way to be invisible for that long."

Mika drummed her finger for a minute, contemplating. "I don't know about this shit…"

"Bitch, what's to know?" her cousin demanded. "You gettin' a muthafuckin' place to live, rent free, with free utilities."

"Yeah, but I just got back in town. I don't wanna start off doin' any hardcore gangsta shit."

"You ain't doin' nuthin' but bein' a fuckin' mailman – stickin' a package in a damn box, basically. What's hardcore or gangsta about that?"

"It's all the shit surrounding the delivery that's screaming 'gangsta,' like the fact that I don't know what's in the package. I don't know who's calling for it. I don't know who's picking it up. There's a lot of fuckin' unknowns here, and that makes me nervous."

Nay-Nay sat quietly for a moment, then let out a deep breath. "Just think about it for a second, cuz. You got one job that may take a minute of your time once or twice a week. Whether it's hood shit or not, that's easy. On top of that – and this was meant to be a surprise – you'll be collecting a few bucks as well."

Mika's eyebrows went up. "Really?"

"Yeah, really," Nay-Nay said. "But I had give to Willie a monster blowjob to get the cash tacked on."

"The fuck you talkin' about?" Mika shot back. "You suck that muthafucka off every night anyway."

"Yeah, but this time I let him cum in my mouth," her cousin said, and they both started laughing.

"Anyway," Nay-Nay went on after they regained their composure, "You wanna do this shit or not?"

Looking around the place, Mika slowly nodded. "Yeah, I'm in."

"Good," Nay-Nay said, handing her the apartment keys. "There's just one other thing: don't fuck with the package. I know it'll be tempting with Christmas right around the corner and shit, but don't try to guess what's inside it, unwrap it, or peek inside it. Muthafuckas at the top of the food chain will not be pleased with that shit. Ya feel me?"

Mika nodded. "I'm wicha."

"Alright," her cousin said with a smile. "Now let's go get a fuckin' drink to celebrate yo ho-ass bein' back in town."

SHE'S HIS DRUG, HE'S HER THUG

Chapter 3

"What da fuck?!" Mika screamed, trying to make herself heard over the music. "I don't remember it bein' this damn loud in here!"

"Sound the same as always to me!" Nay-Nay shouted back.

They were sitting in a booth at Shakers, one of their favorite nightclub spots. (The name supposedly alluded to the fact that the place was always full of rump shakers.) Mika was happy to be out – she really hadn't been to a club since before going on the run – but apparently she'd lost her appreciation for loud music. Still, she was grateful to her cousin for helping her get back into the swing of things.

After Nay-Nay had mentioned getting a drink earlier, Mika was down for that shit but wanted to get cleaned up first. She had spent over a day traveling (having to switch fuckin' buses and all) and wanted – no *needed* – to take a shower before she did anything else.

So, while she got cleaned up, Nay-Nay had run out to a chicken spot and got them something to eat. She was back by the time Mika was out the shower. After wolfing that shit down (Mika couldn't remember the last time she'd had any fried bird), they'd gone to Nay-Nay's place to change clothes – no way was Mika gonna wear any of that shit out that she'd been hauling around for months. Luckily, she and Nay-Nay were about the same size, so her cousin's clothes were a close fit.

Ultimately, she chose a black tube top and a pair of form-fitting jeans, while her cousin squeezed into a red, strapless mini dress. Thirty minutes later, they were in Shakers, sliding into a booth (which they were lucky to get on a Friday night).

"You good?" Nay-Nay asked.

"Huh?" Mika said, leaning close to hear over the music.

"I asked if you were good," her cousin said. "You bein' kinda quiet. You tired?"

Mika shook her head. "Naw – I slept on the bus. I'm good."

"Alright, I'm gonna go get us some drinks."

"Thanks, cuz."

Nay-Nay just nodded in response as she slid out of the booth and then sashayed up to the bar. Mika noticed that she didn't take her purse, credits cards or cash – hell, as far as Mika knew, she hadn't even brought any of that shit. That being the case, she just watched as her cousin worked her magic.

There was a line at the bar, and Nay-Nay tapped the shoulder of a guy in front of her and said something to him – probably asking some bullshit, like how long he'd been in line. The guy eyed Nay-Nay liked she was an ice cream cone he wanted to lick all night long, but managed to say something in response. Her cousin smiled at the dude and said something back, then laughed out loud at the guy's reply.

Mika stopped paying at that point, knowing what was next: by the time they got to the front of the line, Nay-Nay would have that nigga eating out of her hand. After that, he'd be picking up their tab all night long, if they let him.

This was routine for Mika and Nay-Nay – only dumb bitches bought their own drinks at a place like Shakers. Even ugly-ass hoes could get a nigga to pay if they worked their shit right. Of course, that usually meant the muthafucka buying was ugly, too, but sometimes you had to do ugly. (And when the lights were out, looks didn't always matter, as long as the nigga had bomb-ass dick.)

On this particular occasion, Nay-Nay did good from the standpoint of looks. As expected, she came back to the table a few minutes later with drinks in hand, and the nigga from the bar following her like a lost puppy that had finally found his momma. He wasn't bad-looking, and had a cute friend as well.

Nay-Nay put a drink on the table in front of her, saying, "Mika, this is Carlos" – she gestured towards the nigga from the bar – "and Jeff."

The two men gave perfunctory greetings as Nay-Nay slid into the booth next to Mika. It was a subtle indication that Jeff and Carlos should join them, which they did, with the former sitting across from Mika while the latter faced Nay-Nay.

At that point, the small talk fuckin' ensued. Turned out Carlos was a factory worker and Jeff was in construction. Like every other nigga in the hood, both had aspirations of being rappers. (Carlos even spat out a weak-ass rhyme about having a pimped-out ride and mansion, which Nay-Nay acted as though she liked.)

After a few minutes, Carlos leaned across the table and said something to Nay-Nay that Mika didn't catch. Her cousin smiled and nodded, then turned to Mika and leaned towards her ear.

"Hey, I'm gonna step outside for a minute," she said.

"The fuck, Nay?!" Mika hissed. "You been knowing this nigga five minutes!"

"Chill, bitch," Nay-Nay said. "I'm just gonna smoke a little something out in his car."

"Yeah, I bet you gone smoke something – smoke his fuckin' pole!"

"Fuck you," her cousin muttered angrily. "Ya know what? Fine – we'll keep our black asses in here." Turning to Carlos, she said, "You wanna dance?"

Nay-Nay had asked it like a question, but didn't really give Carlos a chance to respond. Instead she just slid out the booth, grabbed his hand, and dragged his ass out to the dance floor.

"How 'bout you?" Jeff asked a few seconds later. "Wanna dance?"

"Not really," Mika answered, still looking at her cousin and Carlos dancing.

"It's cool," Jeff said with a nod. "I'm not really feelin' you either."

Mika's head suddenly snapped in Jeff's direction. What the fuck did he mean, he wasn't feeling her? She could have anybody in this bitch she wanted! She could have that nigga begging for just a whiff of her pussy inside a minute if she chose to.

Rather than respond, Mika slid out the booth and headed to the dance floor. Once there, she turned to face the booth, where Jeff was still sitting, making sure he could see her. She closed her eyes for a moment, just feeling the music. It was a popular rap song, one with a catchy hook and a nice bass you could feel moving damn near through your whole fuckin' body.

Eyes still closed, Mika started dancing, moving in time to the music. She let her hips sway side-to-side at first, then she went into her signature move: a hip roll that was provocative as fuck, guaranteed to get a nigga's dick hard. She started getting into it then, raising her hands up and rocking her upper body while her hips continued to move.

Still dancing, she opened her eyes; just as she expected, Jeff was watching – looking at her like she was the only woman on the planet.

Bet you feelin' me now, *muthafucka*, she thought, smiling to herself as she put her hands on her waist and went down low, still rolling her hips. Then she turned around and started twerking, letting him get a good look at that ass.

Suddenly, Mika felt somebody come up behind her. They didn't touch her, but she knew they were there – it was that sense you get when someone steps inside your personal space. Thinking it was Jeff, she stopped twerking and went back to her hip roll, straightening up and turning around. Much to her surprise, it wasn't Jeff who'd stepped to her on the dance floor. It was some dyke.

The woman looked like she was in her early twenties, with large, dreamy eyes and big, pouty lips that currently sported dark red lipstick. Her eyebrows were thick and well-manicured, and her hair – cut down into a low fade and dyed blond – seemed perfectly contrasted against her flawless, light-brown complexion.

Lesbian or not, she was one of the most beautiful women Mika had ever seen. In fact, she probably would have had every nigga in the place tripping over their dicks to get to her, if not for the fact that she was wearing overalls and men's work boots.

The woman still hadn't touched her, but she had started dancing in a way (and giving Mika a look) that made it clear that she was open to the idea of them getting to know each other – at least on the dance floor.

For Mika, it wasn't the first time a dyke had seemingly been attracted to her. But, although she'd admittedly done some freaky things with women, she really didn't roll like that. She was strictly dickly, and she was about to tell the blonde dyke that when she decided to have a little fun.

Momentarily glancing at Jeff to make sure he was still watching, Mika turned her attention back to the dyke, gave her a thousand-watt smile, and started dancing with her. The woman grinned back, showing teeth that were white and perfect, obviously happy that her unstated invitation to dance had been well-received.

It became evident almost immediately that, despite the boots and overalls, the dyke could really dance. More importantly, she was respectful. Unlike most niggas, who start grinding on you the second you start dancing (like they trying to fuck you through your clothes), the woman got close but didn't actually make contact of any sort. It was Mika who took the initiative, stepping in and pressing her hips to the dyke's (who started grinning even more broadly).

The woman put a hand on Mika's hips, but Mika immediately grabbed it and moved it down to her ass while putting her arms around the lesbian's neck. They continued grinding for a few seconds, then Mika stepped back, spun around and began twerking again, letting the dyke get right up on her ass. She didn't need to see it to know that the dyke was back there acting like she was pounding that ass from behind.

Mika straightened up and then turned to face her dance partner again. This time, the dyke didn't wait for an invitation. As Mika put her arms up around the woman's neck again, the lesbian put one hand on Mika's hip but let the other slide up to Mika's tits, giving one of them a firm but gentle squeeze.

SHE'S HIS DRUG, HE'S HER THUG

Mika let out a slight gasp. She wasn't wearing a bra, and the squeeze had caught her a little by surprise. Before she knew it, the dyke had her hand under the tube top, circling the areola of one tit, tweaking the nipple of the other, then repeating the action. In no time at all, Mika's nipples were like fucking nailheads.

Maybe this was a mistake, Mika thought, *dancing with this dyke.* She noted, however, that her tits were strongly disagreeing with her. (But that shouldn't have been surprising. The dyke had probably touched thousands of tits in her day. At this point, she should be a like a fucking drill sergeant when it came to nipples and shit, making them bitches stand at attention with a word.)

Fortunately, from the way they were dancing, it wasn't likely that anyone had noticed what was happening. And if they did, it wouldn't be that unusual. There was usually all kinds of grab-ass taking place on the dance floor. (One time, this couple had even started fucking out there. Nobody probably would have noticed – would have just assumed they were having a heavy grinding session – but the woman had started moaning and screaming "Harder! Fuck me harder!")

Mika wasn't about to start saying anything like that, but that shit *was* feeling good. That said, getting busy with the dyke wasn't in the cards as far as she was concerned, but the action with her tits was making her cognizant of the fact that she hadn't gotten laid in a while, and making it a lot more likely that she'd go home with some nigga tonight and fuck the shit outta him. (And in the back of her mind, she was grateful that she'd managed to stay on the pill during those months on the run.)

The song ended, bringing Mika back to herself. She touched the dyke's arm and the woman immediately and inconspicuously withdrew her hand. Mika gave her a smile and walked away, heading back towards the booth.

Jeff, she noticed, looked like he didn't know which way was up. Mika smiled, knowing that he was wishing he could take back what he'd said about not being into her. She was sweating a little from dancing, but knew she still looked good – especially with her nipples about to punch holes through that thin-ass top. More to the point, there wasn't a nigga alive who could watch her dancing and not think – no, *dream* – about tapping that ass.

"Hey," said a husky voice from behind her, just as she reached the booth. "Any chance I could buy you a drank?"

Spinning around, Mika saw the dyke she'd just been dancing with standing there.

"Excuse me?" Mika muttered.

"I wanted to know if I could buy you a drank," the woman repeated.

Mika contemplated for a minute. If it had been a man asking her, she probably would have said "Yes." But considering what had just happened on the dance floor, she didn't want to lead the woman on. All Mika had been trying to do was make that nigga Jeff eat crow, and she knew lesbian shit got most men excited (although who the fuck knew why).

"Thanks," Mika began, "but, uh–"

Mika found herself cut off as someone shouted, "Sheree, what da fuck you thank you doin'?"

Mika looked towards the sound of the voice and saw a woman there about her own age, wearing a spaghetti-strap white tank top and black pants. She was staring at the dyke – Sheree – and looking furious.

"Huh?" said Sheree. "Tonya, baby, whachu talkin' 'bout?"

"Don't 'baby' me," Tonya shot back. "I come in here looking for you, and you all up on *this* ho!"

As she finished speaking, she gestured towards Mika, who immediately flew into a rage.

"Bitch, who you callin' a ho?!" Mika demanded.

"Ho, who you callin' a bitch?" Tonya said in response.

"I know you not callin' *me* a ho!" Mika argued.

"Who da fuck it look like I'm talkin' 'bout, ho?" Tonya replied, hand on her hip and rolling her neck.

Mika turned to the dyke she'd been dancing with. "You better put yo bitch in check before her ass wake up in traction."

"Bitch!" Tonya shouted, starting to step in Mika's direction. "Don't you know I wi–"

She didn't get any further as Sheree jumped in front of her, gripped her arms, and started pushing her away, saying, "Come on, baby, don't start nuthin'. Me and her was just talkin'…"

Although she allowed herself to be shoved away, Tonya kept glowering at Mika, who shouted, "Yeah, bitch – take yo ass on 'fo you get fucked up!" She then turned and picked up the glass holding what was left of her drink, wanting to take a sip after her exertions on the dance floor.

"What was that shit about?" asked a voice next to her.

Mika turned and saw that Nay-Nay was back from the dance floor with Carlos. She'd been so focused on that bitch Tonya that she hadn't even noticed when they came back.

"Just some lez bitch, actin' like I wanted to steal her dyke girlfriend," Mika replied.

"What, again?" her cousin asked with a grin.

"Fuck you, bitch," Mika replied, snickering. "That shit's only happened like once – no, *twice* – before."

Giggling, Nay-Nay looked like she wanted to say something else, but was cut off by a yell. Turning towards the sound, Mika saw that Tonya had broken away from Sheree (knocked the blonde dyke down, in fact). Screaming in fury, she charged straight at Mika.

Mika reacted almost instinctively, throwing her drink into Tonya's face. Reflexively, Tonya closed her eyes and checked her speed, which was all the opening Mika needed.

Still holding her drink glass, Mika smashed it into the side of Tonya's head. The glass didn't break (not immediately, anyway), but Tonya dropped to the floor, obviously stunned. The drink glass landed next to her, shattering in the process and sending pieces of glass and ice cascading across the floor. Mika ignored that shit; instead, she stepped over and kicked Tonya in the side – hard. Tonya winced in pain and Mika kicked her again. Before she could get a third kick in, her cousin was in front of her.

Nay-Nay was shouting something, probably telling her to back off, but Mika couldn't really hear her. All she was focused on was Tonya, whose girlfriend Sheree was now racing over.

Apparently, however, it was Bad-Luck-Dyke-Night at Shakers, because Sheree stepped on what looked like a piece of glass or ice, and the next thing you know her legs went flying out from under her. She hit the floor like she'd been body-slammed, and simply lay there moaning.

Mika barely noticed Sheree, though. Tonya was still the center of her universe, and she was on the verge of stomping her ass in the face when – much like the attack she'd suffered in the alley – stout arms as thick as oak trees closed around her from behind and lifted her off the floor. A minute later, she found herself unceremoniously dumped outside on the sidewalk by a huge bouncer.

Moments later, a second bouncer dragged her cousin out, who was shouting, "Why y'all throwin' *me* out?! I ain't even do shit! Y'all muthafuckas wrong for this!"

Ignoring her, another bouncer tossed them Nay-Nay's coat and Mika's jacket, respectively, both of which they had left in the booth.

Still indignant, Nay-Nay yelled, "Y'all need to be tossing them other bitches out, not us! They the ones startin' shit!"

"People are always arguing," said one of the bouncers. "Club policy is that the one who starts the *physical* fight is who gets shown the door."

"Well, we ain't just gonna stand there and let bitches talk shit to us," Nay-Nay declared, "so y'all need to change that policy."

"We'll take it under advisement," said the bouncer before going back inside.

Nay-Nay and Mika looked at each other, and then burst out laughing.

"Bitch, you ain't changed a bit while I was gone," Mika stated, still giggling.

"You neither," said her cousin, and they both started laughing again.

Chapter 4

Nay-Nay wanted to hit another club, but Mika took the incident at Shakers as a sign. She told her cousin she was calling it a night.

"I been back in town less than a day," she said, "and I'm already beefin' with bitches – and over a dyke, at that!"

Nay-Nay was obviously still in a clubbing mood, but reluctantly drove her back to the projects. As Mika got out the car, her cousin said, "Alright, be good. And don't forget what I said about that phone call you gone get."

"I ain't forgot," Mika assured her, then shut the door.

As Mika headed for the entry of the projects, her cousin stayed out front, waiting. As always, there was a bunch of niggas hanging around the front of the building, and tonight was no different. They were all over the courtyard of the complex to be honest, standing everywhere from the sidewalk to the side of the building. More to the point, it was always like this – there was always somebody out here twenty-four seven.

That said, not all of them were out there being fuckin' idle. A lot of these niggas had jobs (in the loosest sense of the word.) Some of them were runners, some of them lookouts, some of them just wannabes…

All of this flitted through her head as she took the walkway to the building entrance, ignoring all the Hey-Shawty's and Damn-you-fine-Momma's she heard en route. When she reached the door she turned and waved to her cousin as she stepped in, letting her know she'd at least made it inside okay. Nay-Nay then honked before pulling off, while Mika headed to the elevator. Five minutes later, she was in her apartment.

She immediately went to the sofa, kicking off her shoes. She spent a moment stretching out her legs and then relaxed. For the first time in what seemed like forever, she was going to go to sleep and wake up in a bed. She was going to be able to go the bathroom without passing through a common area. She wouldn't have to wait in line to use a communal shower. She'd always felt that living in the hood was shitty – and it was – but she now knew that it was possible to do a lot fuckin' worse.

Grabbing her shoes, she began heading for the bedroom when something near the kitchen caught her eye. It was a flashing red dot on the answering machine.

Someone had called while she was out.

Chapter 5

Whoever it was, they had called four times: twice in quick succession about an hour earlier (probably assumed they had dialed wrong the first time), then a third time fifteen minutes later, and a fourth time fifteen minutes after that.

The Caller ID identified the caller as "Anonymous." It was probably someone on a burner and using the prepaid phone's Caller ID Block, although that probably wasn't necessary. You could pay cash for a burner and not have to give out any info about yourself. That being the case, you didn't have waste time blocking your ID because none that info was on the phone anyway.

Worried about having missed the call, Mika jettisoned her initial plan to jump in the shower and go to bed. Instead, she stayed up for a bit, just in case they called back. But sitting staring at the phone was boring as fuck, so while she was waiting she pulled out her cell phone and called her oldest brother, DeMarcus.

When Mika had left, it had pretty much been with just the clothes on her back. However, while she was on that first bus out of town, she had called DeMarcus and asked him to swing by her place and pack up her shit. It was mostly clothes, although she'd also had a TV and a couple of appliances and electronics. Her brother had complied (although he'd had to wait until she mailed him the key), and had since been storing her stuff at his place. Now that she was back, though (and likely to stay), she realized needed to get her shit.

DeMarcus answered on the second ring. They chatted for a few minutes before Mika got down to business, and in no time at all had secured a promise from her brother to bring her stuff by first thing in the morning.

Satisfied, she quickly got off the phone, then spent another ten minutes waiting before deciding to risk taking a quick shower. Afterwards, she spent another quarter-hour on standby before calling it quits for the night.

Mika went to the bedroom and stretched out on the bed, reflecting for a moment on how good it felt to be back (and to be staying some place other than a shelter, or a room that felt like a tin can). However, she must have been a lot more tired than she thought, because she was knocked out within five minutes, falling asleep with the lights still on. Although she slept fitfully, she didn't wake up until the next morning when the phone started ringing.

It was *them*.

SHE'S HIS DRUG, HE'S HER THUG

Chapter 6

Needless to say, Mika didn't know who "they" were and was actually dead to the fuckin' world when the phone started ringing.

The first ring woke her up, and for a second she was completely fucking confused – had no idea where she was and wasn't sure she wasn't dreaming. It took her a moment to get her bearings, to recall where the fuck she was and what she was doing there, and by that time the phone had rang a second time.

Something clicked in her mind at that point; the mental fog lifted, and everything suddenly became clear.

Oh shit! She screamed at herself, eyes going wide as saucers. *The phone!*

A moment later, she was streaking towards the other room like a muthafuckin' track star trying to win a gold medal at the Olympics. The phone rang a third time just before she got there. She snatched the phone – a wireless model – out of the base like it had stole something from her and switched it on.

"Hello?" Mika muttered into the phone. "Hello?"

"Turn the muhfuckin' machine off," said a gruff male voice.

At that moment, Mika realized that the answering machine had switched on, presumably after the third ring. It was now issuing a slight, staticky hiss, indicating that the current conversation was being recorded.

Mika looked at the phone base, which – in addition to serving as a charger for the phone – housed the answering machine. She had no fuckin' clue how the thing operated. After a few seconds of randomly pushing buttons that looked like they might have an effect (and getting nothing but some odd-ass beeps for her trouble), she finally gave up and was about to just yank the fucking cord out the wall when it seemingly shut off on its own.

Somewhat satisfied, she turned her attention back to her caller and spoke into the phone. "Hello?"

"'Bout fuckin' time," grumbled the caller. "We'll be there at nine for the shit. Have yo ass in position."

"Okay," she muttered. "The, uh… It'll be in the, uh… It'll be in the designated spot."

"Naw, fuck dat. Just hold it 'til we get there."

Mika's mouth almost fell open.

"Huh?" she mumbled. "No, no, no! That's not what I was told. They told me there's a procedure, and I'm sup–"

"Fuck procedure," her caller said. "We'll be there at nine, so see you then." There was a moment of silence, and then the caller added, "Don't make us come looking for you."

There was an ominous tone to the caller's voice during his last statement, and it was so chilling that Mika continued holding the phone to her ear for a full thirty seconds before she finally realized he had hung up.

****

"What da fuck, Nay-Nay!" Mika screamed into the phone. "This is exactly the kinda shit I said I didn't wanna get involved in."

"Just calm down, Mika," her cousin said. "It ain't that serious."

"Are you fuckin' listenin' to me?" Mika spat back. "These niggas talkin' about comin' up in here. That sound serious as a muthafucka to me."

43

"What's her fuckin' problem?" asked someone in the background at Nay-Nay's place.

Mika recognized Willie's voice, and knew he was probably pissed – not just because she didn't want to deal with handing off any packages, but also because it was early as hell on a Saturday morning. Mika had gotten the call just after six o'clock, and she had immediately called Nay-Nay afterwards in an attempt to sort shit out.

"Look, let me handle this," her cousin said to Willie, who mumbled something back. Speaking again to Mika, she said, "Alright, this ain't how it was s'posed to happen, but it ain't a big deal."

"Forgive me," Mika retorted, "but I think it's a big fuckin' deal when I'm s'posed to let some niggas I don't know into an apartment where I'm staying by myself as part of some shady deal. This is how bitches end up in landfills."

"Tell that ho ain't nuthin' gonna happen to her," Willie said in the background. "The dumb bitch just need to handle up."

"Hold on, muthafucka," Nay-Nay said, obviously talking to her boyfriend. "This my cousin you talkin' 'bout, not yo crackhead mammy. So I suggest you check yo tone, or you can try sucking yo *own* dick tonight."

Willie mumbled something that Mika didn't catch, but to which her cousin replied, "That's what I fuckin' thought." Getting back on the phone, she said, "Listen, Mika. I prolly should have told you, but sometimes it does go down this way – you gotta meet these niggas in person. But it's always cool, nuthin' happens. I've done it myself."

"What?" Mika blurted out.

"I said, I've had to do this shit myself," Nay-Nay stated, "in that same apartment where you at. Nuthin' ever happens."

Mika just held the phone, still upset and not saying anything. She'd known she was getting involved in something shady when she agreed to the deal with the apartment, but she had expected to be on the periphery. This was putting her smack in the middle of what was probably a fuckin' drug deal.

"Look," her cousin went on, "You know I wouldn't have put you over there if I thought there was any chance of sommin' happenin' to you. You know that, right?"

Mika let out a deep breath, "Yeah."

"And I damn sho wouldn't have made the offer if I thought you couldn't handle it, would I?"

"Naw."

"Alright then," Nay-Nay chirped. "Like I said, before, nuthin's gonna happen. You got this, cuz."

"We'll see," Mika said. "But if this shit goes sideways and these muthafuckas carve me up, I want my tombstone to say 'This Nay-Nay fault...'"

Chapter 7

The call with her cousin helped Mika feel a little grounded again, but she still wasn't at ease. She really didn't want to get caught up in anything dealing with hard drugs. Sure, she liked to party – liked to get her drink on, occasionally smoked some weed – but she typically avoided the hardcore shit on all fronts. She'd seen too many people get fucked up by becoming addicted or get killed from dealing. Now here she was, in the middle of some fucked up transaction that she actually wanted no part of.

Whachu expect, bitch? asked the voice in her head. *You gettin' free digs and some cash on the side for deliverin' a package – whachu you think was goin' on?*

Mika was still mentally chastising herself when a knock sounded at the door, startling her. She looked at her watch and saw that it was only eight o'clock. She'd been so distraught over the phone call that she hadn't even noticed the time, which had flown by. She hadn't even gotten dressed yet (unless you counted the sweats that doubled as pajamas).

The knock sounded again, louder. Mika shook her head in disbelief. Ninety-nine point nine-nine-nine percent of the time, niggas are late for their own funeral. The one time she'd love for a muthafucka to be late, they show up an hour early. She checked to make sure she had Pierce in her pocket – if she went down, she was going to go down swinging – and then went to the door. She risked glancing through the peephole as whoever it was knocked a third time, then sighed in relief. A moment later she unlocked the door, opened it, and let her brother Demarcus in.

"Damn girl, were you sleep?" he asked as he entered, carrying a suitcase in each hand and a duffel bag

46

slung on his back – all of which she recognized as her luggage from her old apartment.

"No," she answered, closing the door while her brother set everything down.

"Well, gimme a hug," he said, grinning as he spread his arms.

Mika smiled and stepped forward, giving him a quick squeeze and getting one in return. Oddly enough, it made her feel better. DeMarcus wasn't just her oldest brother; at times, he had practically been a parent to her and their siblings – depending on what was going on in their lives at the time. Basically, he'd been her rock on too many occasions to count.

"Alright, I ain't gonna act like I did some great packing job," he admitted. "I basically just threw yo shit in these bags" – he gestured towards the suitcases – "and that's where they been the past few months. Pretty much everything should be in there."

"Pretty much?" she repeated skeptically. "What the fuck does that mean?"

He glanced at the floor for a moment. "Serena may have gone through your stuff once or twice looking for something to wear."

"You better be lyin'," his sister said. "You let your fuckin' klepto girlfriend go through my shit?"

"No, I didn't *let* her," he insisted, "but she fuckin' lives with me and I can't watch her all the time. But she always washed and put your stuff back when she was finished – plus I didn't think you'd mind."

"Normally I wouldn't, but the bitch is a klepto."

"No, she ain't, and I wish you'd stop saying that."

"Fine, she's not a klepto," Mika conceded. "She just like takin' shit that don't belong to her."

47

"'Cause that shit never happens in the hood, right? Nobody round this muthafucka ever takes shit that don't belong to them. They all fuckin' model citizens."

"Compared to that bitch they are, because if they steal from you they not bold enough to flaunt that shit in yo face."

DeMarcus stared at her for a moment. "This 'bout yo necklace, ain't it?"

"You mean my necklace that came up missin' after we all went to the pool, and a week later yo girlfriend shows up with one just like it?" Mika asked.

"She told you soon as she saw it that she had one just like it," DeMarcus reminded her.

"That's called manufacturin' an alibi – like one of those niggas on true crime shows, tellin' five-oh how they told their wife to get the brakes checked, knowin' all the while that they cut that bitch brake line."

Demarcus crossed his arms. "You wanna just go through yo shit? See what's missin' and send me a fuckin' bill?"

Mika simply stared at him for a moment, then let out a deep breath. "Sorry. I've just got some shit on my mind. I been back in town like a day and already got shit poppin' off. But it's cool if Serena wore some of my stuff."

"Cool, I'll let her know," DeMarcus said. "And yeah, the bitch *is* a klepto."

They both laughed at that. Gaining her composure a few seconds later, Mika looked again at the stuff her brother had brought in and then frowned.

"So where's my *other* stuff," she asked. "Back at your place?"

DeMarcus looked confused. "What other stuff?"

"Well, I had more than just clothes. I had a TV, phone, and other shit."

"Oh," her brother muttered, brow creasing "About that…"

"What about it?" Mika asked, her curiosity piqued.

"Well, when you left, it was like the beginnin' of the month. Rent was already paid, so it seemed like a crime to let that muthafucka go to waste."

"What did you do?"

"I knew a nigga who needed a place, but wasn't in the market for anything long-term. We worked out a deal."

"And?" Mika asked, knowing there was more.

"There's no 'and.' I mean, nuthin' *bad* – the shit worked out good. I got almost a full month's rent just for lettin' him stay there two weeks."

"Two weeks?" Mika repeated, skeptically. "He paid that much for two weeks? What the fuck was he doin' in there, makin' Christy?"

DeMarcus didn't say anything, just gave her a blank look.

"Nigga, you better be jokin'," she said. "You let some muthafucka turn my place into a meth lab?"

"No," her brother insisted, shaking his head. "I mean, I dunno *exactly* what he was doin', but I really don't thin–"

"Just stop," Mika said, cutting him off. "At least tell me he ain't blow the place up, so I can at least maybe ask for my security deposit back."

"Naw, it's still in one piece, but, uh…you may not get that security deposit back just yet."

Mika looked him up and down. "What da fuck does that mean?"

"Well, the money from that first deal was so good that…well, I sorta kept it goin'."

"Kept *what* going?" Mika asked. "Da fuck you talkin' 'bout?"

"I kinda kept leasing the place – kept paying the rent, but it's still in yo name. But it turned out there's a lot of muthafuckas will pay top dollar to temporarily, kinda, sub-lease a place."

"Oh, I bet there are," Mika said. "Fuckin' meth cooks who'd rather blow up somebody else's apartment than their own. Niggas who cheatin' on they wife and want a secret spot to tap that side-chick ass. Damn prostitutes wanting a cheap place to suck-and-fuck niggas all night long."

Demarcus didn't say immediately say anything. Instead, he reached into a pocket and pulled out a wad of cash bound with a rubber band.

"Your cut," he said.

"Which means you probably got twice as much," his sister quipped as she picked up the cash.

"I'm doin' all the fuckin' work," Demarcus stressed. "Finding people to stay there, paying the rent, cleaning that bitch up every time someone leaves…"

"So, who's there now?" asked Mika.

Her brother shook his head. "Nobody."

"Good," she responded, then held her hand out, palm up. "Gimme my key."

DeMarcus simply stared at her for a minute, then reached into his pocket and pulled out a ring of keys.

"You one cold bitch," her brother said as he removed a key. "Gonna take the business I built up and kick me out."

"Nigga, is you a fool?" she asked as she took her key. "My name is still on the fuckin' lease. If some nigga cookin' up meth and it explodes, or some prostitute get her throat cut up in there, they gone come lookin' for *me*. I don't need that shit."

"Come on, Mika. Ain't nuthin' gone happen."

"Well if that's what you think, why don't you rent out *yo* damn apartment for this shit?"

"What, you think I'm doin' this for *me*? I'm doin' this for *you* – trying to make sure my lil' sister ain't hurtin' for cash."

They both stared at each other for a second, then both burst out laughing.

"Nigga," Mika said, smiling, "you are so fulla shit…"

Chapter 8

DeMarcus stayed only for a few more minutes, then Mika hustled him out. She had shit going down soon and didn't want her brother around, possibly being caught up in some shit he wasn't prepared for. Plus, she needed to get ready.

One of the suitcases her brother had brought in was a midsized expandable upright. It was basic black in color, with wheels, and she quickly took it to the bedroom. Once there, she unzipped it and dumped all the contents on the bed. Next, she felt around the bottom of the suitcase until she found what she was looking for.

Basically, the suitcase had a false bottom. It had been a gift from an ex-boyfriend – a guy who used to take her out of town one or two weekends a month. (He'd gotten her the suitcase after seeing the ratty-looking carry-on she'd originally had and declared that *his* woman deserved something better.) They'd never gone any place special, usually just one of the neighboring cities, but to Mika – who had rarely done any traveling before – it had always been great to get away, even if just for a day or two.

Of course, that was before she found out about the false compartment in the suitcase, and how her boyfriend was using it to transport drugs. In essence, almost the entire time they were together, he was using her as a drug mule. The shit was always in *her* suitcase, so if the cops pulled them over and found it, he could just deny, deny, deny.

The only way she'd found out what he was up to was when she was taking a shower one day and decided – on impulse – to go get him and drag him in with her. So she'd come out the bathroom naked and wet (in more ways than one), only to find that nigga shoving a key of coke into the bottom of her bag. She broke up with that muthafucka a few days later, and shortly thereafter his ass got busted for possession-with-intent-to-distribute. That was strike three for his monkey ass.

Adios, muthafucka! she said to herself, smiling at the memory as she pulled the item she'd been looking for out of the false bottom: a gun.

It was a small automatic, about six inches or so long. Not liking the idea of his little sister being out on her own without protection, Demarcus had gotten it for her when she'd first left home at sixteen – after their mom's latest boyfriend kept coming on to her. (Their mom had always had horrible taste in men and equally bad judgment in that department – letting some of those niggas move in after only knowing them a few days.) Her brother had even taken her out and shown her how to use the gun, although that had required a trip to the fucking woods. Mika would never claim to be a marksman, but she knew the basics – like how to take the safety off, as well as load, aim, and shoot.

Fortunately, she'd never had to use the gun. It was allegedly clean, but her brother had obviously gotten it in the hood, so who the fuck knew? There might be ten bodies on that gun. Thus, she'd pretty much kept it out of sight and at some point had started using the false bottom as the de facto hiding place for it. The plan, of course, had been to only take the gun out for emergencies.

Well, today feels like a fuckin' emergency, she thought.

SHE'S HIS DRUG, HE'S HER THUG

Chapter 9

Mika tucked the gun into the waist of her sweats and pulled the shirt down over it. It felt odd and slightly uncomfortable, but she knew from experience that you could get used to just about anything over time. Plus, she didn't expect to be packing on a regular basis. This was just in case shit with this package got zany for some reason.

Speaking of the package, she finally opened up the cabinet above the fridge and took a look at what all the excitement was about. It turned out to be a plain brown box sealed with packing tape.

As she pulled it down, Mika guessed that it weighed about ten or fifteen pounds. Technically, it wasn't very heavy, but if she was right about what was probably inside, she was in over her head. *Way* over her head.

She placed the box on the kitchen counter and just stared at it for a minute. Shit had gotten real pretty fucking quick, and she was guessing there was either one of two things in the box: either H or blow.

As to the former, Mika knew people who fooled with heroin – both dealers and users – and considered it a cheap drug. That being the case, she was pretty sure that the box contained blow – a couple of keys of coke, at the very least.

She shook her head in damn near disbelief, wondering what the fuck she'd gotten herself into. However, she didn't have time to dwell on it for long, as her thoughts were suddenly interrupted by a loud knocking at the door. Checking the time, she saw that it was pretty much meeting time.

No chance that's DeMarcus this time, she thought.

Taking a deep breath, she went to the door. She spent a moment debating on whether to use the peephole, then decided against it. No matter who she saw on the other side, she was going to have to open the fucking door, so there was no use acting like peeping who was out there was going to give her some options.

Mind made up, she opened the door – and then had to fight to keep her mouth from dropping open.

The guy standing there was the one who'd found her in Tweet's closet.

The one who'd taken her license.

The one she'd been on the run from for damn near half a year.

Kane.

Chapter 10

Mika froze, just starting at Kane, caught completely off guard. Her mind told her to go for the gun, to pull that bitch out and start blasting, but her body wouldn't obey.

On his part, Kane simply stared back, looking her in the eye. After a few seconds, he said, "We s'pose to be doin' this shit in the hallway? Or you expectin' some kind of code word and shit?"

Still stunned, Mika somehow got her legs to move, stepping back and opening the door enough for Kane to come in. That's when she realized something else: he wasn't alone. She'd been so shocked at seeing Kane that she hadn't even noticed that there was another nigga with him – some thug with ink showing around his neck as well as the back of his hands and wrists (which was all she could see because of the bomber jacket he wore). Just looking at those, she already knew without seeing it that he had tats all over. He also had a wicked scar running down one side of his face, and eyes that were constantly scanning the room (not to mention looking over his shoulder). Mika automatically knew the type: ex-con.

Kane glanced around casually, taking in the room. He was dress for the weather, wearing a mid-length black leather coat, gloves, a black turtleneck, and jeans.

Simply judging by his attitude, it quickly became apparent to Mika that he hadn't recognized her. (Maybe it was her hair, which was longer now, giving her a slightly different look.) Or maybe he just didn't remember her. Her recollection was that he'd kept his eyes on her face when she was in Tweet's closet, but maybe she was misremembering. After all, she'd been naked then, and given a choice between looking at a girl's face or a pair of tits (plus her pussy), the vote wouldn't even be close for most niggas.

He don't remember, she finally said to herself, relaxing a little. *Just stay cool and this shit will play out without any issues.*

"Alright, Noose," said Kane, interrupting Mika's thoughts as he unzipped his coat. "Check it out."

The ex-con, Noose, nodded and started walking towards the bedroom. It was enough to snap Mika out of her daze.

"Hold on," she demanded. "Where's he going?"

"Chill, momma," Kane advised. "He just scopin' the place out – makin' sure ain't no nigga gonna come steppin' out the bedroom with a shotgun or some shit like that while we here. You'd be surprised the kind of shit that unfolds in this business."

"And what business is that?"

Kane gave her a skeptical look. "If you askin' that, maybe you shouldn't be here."

"Just to clear, I don't *wanna* be here, so let's just get this over," Mika stated. "Your shit's on the counter."

"Damn," Kane muttered. "A woman who's focused on business. I'm down with that."

"I'd rather you get down the stairs and gone."

Kane laughed – an affable chuckling sound that Mika actually found enjoyable. "That's funny. I like a woman who's funny."

"Then it's too bad that I'm really a man," Mika quipped.

Caught flatfooted, Kane looked at her in surprise for a moment. Then he burst out laughing again. Mika, despite her own best judgment, found herself drawn in and laughing with him a moment later.

SHE'S HIS DRUG, HE'S HER THUG

Whachu doin'? demanded the voice in her head. *Don't be jokin' with this muthafucka! He will ventilate you if he remembers who you are!*

"It's clear," said Noose, his hard-edged voice cutting into any joviality that might have still existed. More to the point, Mika recognized it as belonging to the person she'd spoken with on the phone.

"Alright, let's get to it," Kane said.

As he spoke, he reached into a pocket of the jeans he was wearing. Mika's fought her instinctive reaction, which was to go for the gun. A moment later, she felt tension ease out of her body as Kane pulled out a set of keys.

"Lead the way," he said to her.

Mika turned and went into the kitchen, with the two men following behind her. She pointed to the box, which Kane went towards and – using a key from his keyring – sliced open the tape. He then opened up the box and looked inside.

Unfortunately, Mika wasn't in position to see what he was looking at, but Kane must have been satisfied because he looked at Noose and nodded. Noose stepped forward and pulled a small vial of liquid out of his jacket pocket while Kane turned back to Mika.

"What's he doin'?" she asked as Noose began fiddling around with the packages in the box.

"Just a quick chemical analysis," Kane explained. "Makin' sure that we get what we paid for."

"Look like he need some help," Mika said, noticing that Noose seemed to be manically shaking something in his hand.

"Naw, he got this," Kane retorted. "Plus, it's bad business for both of us to be distracted while we up in here."

Before Mika could respond, Noose let out a heads-up whistle, causing Kane to turn in his direction. Noose then tossed something to him, which Kane caught and then held up. Mika saw that it was the vial Noose had pulled from his pocket, except now the liquid in it had turned blue.

"Looks like we in business," Kane announced before tossing the vial back to Noose.

At that point, Noose, reached into the interior of his bomber jacket and pulled out what appeared to be an empty overnight bag. Using both hands, he flicked it in the air once, opening the bag up, and then placed it on the counter. Next, he began taking rectangular items – all wrapped in plain brown paper – out of the box and placing them in the overnight bag.

While Noose was packing, Kane pulled out a cell phone and made a call. Mika heard it ring twice and then thought she detected a man's voice answering.

"It's me," Kane said. "Yeah, no problem... Yeah... Oh yeah, we tested that shit... Yeah, exactly. Cool..."

With that, he hung up the phone. Turning to face Noose, he asked, "We good?"

Noose, who had just finished packing and zipping up the bag, nodded.

"A'ight, we out," Kane announced.

With that, he and Noose began walking towards the door, with the latter in the lead.

SHE'S HIS DRUG, HE'S HER THUG

Noose had just opened the door and stepped out when Kane said, "Gone down to the car. I wanna chat with our hostess for a sec."

Noose cut his eyes at Mika for a moment and looked like he wanted to say something. Ultimately, however, he just shrugged and left, heading for the stairwell directly across from the apartment. The minute he was into the stairwell, Kane turned to her, smiling in a way that, under other circumstances, might have made her blush.

"So," he began, "I know we ain't spent a lot of time together, but I was wonderin' if you wanna grab sommin' to eat sometime."

"Pass," she said flatly.

"Come on," he pleaded. "You ain't even gonna give a brutha a chance?"

"I don't need to. I'm not interested."

"That's not fair," he whined. "You don't even know me, so how can you say you not interested?"

"That's my point – you don't *me*, so how can stand there claiming that you *are* interested?"

"I just feel like we got a connection."

"Well, consider us *dis*connected."

"Damn, momma – you cold."

"This is actually me being warm and bubbly."

Kane laughed. "See, that's what I like about you. Most girls round here got no sense of humor – it's all I-don't-play and I'm-serious-as-a-heart-attack shit all the time. Can't get these bitches to relax for two seconds."

"Might help if you stopped callin' 'em 'bitches.'"

"Maybe," Kane agreed with a nod, "but then they wouldn't respect me."

Now it was Mika's turn to snicker, and against her better judgment, she found herself actually considering his offer for a second before common sense took hold of her again.

"Look," she finally said. "I appreciate the offer but I just don't–"

"Hey, it's cool," Kane chimed in, cutting her off as he began backing towards the stairwell. "I get it – no means no. But I think we woulda made a nice combination."

"You don't even know me," she said.

"Sure I do," he retorted. "Komika."

Mika blinked, slightly confused. Nobody ever called her by her formal, given name. She was always just 'Mika.' It's how she was always introduced, it's how she signed shit, it was what she put on job applications. Her given name usually only came into play with serious shit: taxes, bank accounts, official ID…

Oh shit! She thought, eyes widening. *My driver's license!*

Kane didn't immediately say anything. Instead, he just gave her a knowing smile as he opened the stairwell door. If Mika had any doubt that he remembered her, it was erased by what he said a moment later.

"By the way," Kane added as he stepped into the stairwell. "As odd as it may sound, I think you look just as good with your clothes *on*."

He then gave her a wink and turned to go down the stairs.

At that moment, there was a booming in the stairwell like a cannon going off. At the same time, a chunk of wall next to Kane's head was blown away, making him flinch.

SHE'S HIS DRUG, HE'S HER THUG

Mika instinctively knew what she was hearing and seeing.

Gunfire!

SHE'S HIS DRUG, HE'S HER THUG

Chapter 11

Kane whipped out a gun from somewhere and began returning fire. Mika, across the hall from him, couldn't see who he was shooting at, but didn't want or need to. It wasn't the kind of shit that piqued her interest.

Instinct took over, causing her to duck before scrambling back into the apartment and slamming the door. The gunplay seemed to be taking place in the stairwell so she hadn't been directly in the line of fire, but there was no need to take chances. Bullets ricochet all the fucking time.

Once in the apartment she continued crouching and moved away from the door. With gunshots booming in the stairwell, the same scene was probably playing out on damn near every floor in the tenement, with people scrambling for cover, trying to figure out what the fuck was going on.

Mentally, Mika cussed Nay-Nay out, calling her every name she could imagine.

Bitch, she thought. *Ho. Skank...*

Again, this was exactly the type of fucked-up situation she'd been trying to avoid. Even worse, somehow the shit had not only elevated beyond anything she'd ever imagined, it had gotten completely out of control.

All of this flitted through her mind while the shooting was going on. The gunfire lasted for maybe ten seconds, but felt a hell of a lot longer. When it stopped, she still stayed low for maybe half a minute, then crept quietly to the door. She didn't hear anything, but didn't want to risk putting her eye to the peephole.

Fuck this! she finally said to herself. *I'm outta this bitch!*

SHE'S HIS DRUG, HE'S HER THUG

She opened the door, preparing to run, only to have Kane fall forward into her arms.

SHE'S HIS DRUG, HE'S HER THUG

Chapter 12

Mika wasn't sure how (or why), but she caught the nigga before he hit the floor. He groaned in pain, and his gun clattered as it fell from his hand and landed by his foot.

She wasn't immediately sure of what to do, but Mika knew one thing: she wasn't going to stand there with the door open knowing there was an active shooter in the building. (Then again, they were in the hood. There were probably ten active shooters on every floor of the building, depending on how you defined it.)

Mind made up, she dragged Kane fully inside. She then lowered him to the floor before shutting and locking the door.

Kane moaned, getting her attention, and she took a second to eye him from head to foot. It was hard to tell because his turtleneck was black, but it looked like the shirt was getting soaked with blood. At a guess, he'd probably been shot somewhere in the torso.

Before she knew it — and without consciously having made the decision — she was on the floor next to him, lifting up his shirt. The next moment, he was gripping her wrist, pulling her hand away.

He had a grip that was surprisingly strong for a guy who'd been shot, and Mika gasped a little. She looked at his face and saw anger there, as well as suspicion (and maybe even a little fear). Of course — he'd just been ambushed, and didn't know if she was in on it.

"Nigga, I'm trying to help you!" she hissed, answering his unasked question.

He still looked suspicious, but let her hand go. She pulled up the turtleneck, along with a white-t-shirt underneath. Or rather, it had been a white t-shirt. At the moment it was stained red with blood. However, she did see now that he'd been shoot in the stomach, and – while blood wasn't gushing out in a fountain – she knew he was losing way more than what was healthy.

She was no expert, but a quick body check convinced her that he hadn't caught a slug anywhere else. (Considering it callous, she pushed to the back of her mind the chiseled pecs and well-defined abs she'd noticed while searching for other wounds.)

"Okay, you been shot in the stomach," Mika said to him, although she wasn't sure if he heard her because he seemed to be passing in and out of consciousness.

"Really?" he muttered sarcastically. "Had no...idea..."

"Still trying to be funny, I see. But we gotta get you to a hospital."

"No!" he said forcefully, his eyes snapping open and drilling into her. "Gotta...get outta...here." He then struggled to get up, pretty much unsuccessfully.

"You gotta stay still," Mika argued, repeating shit she'd seen on TV.

"Can't," Kane insisted, shaking his head. "Shooters...be back."

"Oh, shit!" Mika uttered, almost in shock. She hadn't even thought about that.

Chapter 13

Mika scrambled up from the floor and made a mad dash to the bathroom. She then washed her hands furiously before checking to make sure there was no blood on her clothes. Then she raced through the apartment getting together all the shit she considered essential: her wallet, keys, cellphone, etc. She wanted to throw together a bag of clothes, but wasn't sure that she had time. Abandoning the idea, she threw on her jacket and headed towards the door. All in all, it had been less than a minute since Kane had mentioned the shooters coming back.

She had just put her hand on the knob and was preparing to unlock the door when Kane moaned. Reflexively, she looked back at him. He looked like he was half out of it, and obviously in pain (although, from the looks of his stomach – probably not for much longer).

Looking at him now, Mika experienced an odd sense of déjà vu. This was almost the exact same scenario she'd been in five months before – running off helter-skelter from an apartment where someone had been shot (except Tweet had actually been dead instead of just dying).

Back then, Kane could have shot her between the eyes and left her body to rot there in that closet. Hell, most niggas in his position probably would have. But he hadn't. He'd let her live – hadn't even come after her as far as she knew. But now, with their positions somewhat reversed, she had a choice to make.

"Muthafucka…" she muttered, then took off her jacket and ran back to the bathroom.

She had a cheap-ass bath towel that she'd bought from a dollar-store while on the run. It was about as thick as single-ply toilet tissue, but was all she had that might serve. Grabbing it, she ran back to Kane.

It took a little bit of effort, but she eventually got him up on his feet and then wrapped the towel around him in the area of his wound. It wasn't as pretty as when they did it in the movies, but hopefully it would keep him from bleeding out (for which the muthafucka should be grateful). She then pulled his shirt down over the towel and zipped his coat up.

Leaving him braced against a wall, she went back to the bathroom one last time to get cleaned up before putting her jacket back on.

"Ready?" she asked.

"Wait," he murmured. "Gun."

Mika looked down and retrieved his gun from where it had fallen. She was going to pocket it, but Kane held out a hand, indicating that he wanted to hold it. She didn't think it was a good idea, but didn't feel they had time to argue so she handed it over.

"'Kay," Kane he muttered with a nod. "I'm ready."

Mika moved next to him and draped his arm over her shoulder, noticing that he winced as she did so. Moving towards the door, she suddenly realized that she was going to have to bear a good bit of his weight, but there was nothing to be done about that. She then opened the door and they shuffled out into the hallway.

Chapter 14

Much to Mika's surprise, they made it out of the building pretty much without issue. Her first inclination had been to take the elevator downstairs, but Kane had vetoed that. Elevators in the projects were notorious for breaking down, and the last thing they needed was to be stuck between floors with him hampered by a serious wound. (It also made them easy pickings if someone was waiting for them in the lobby.)

The next option had been the stairwell across from the apartment, but the minute she opened the door Mika knew that wasn't an option. Not only was there blood on the floor where Kane had been shot, but she also blood splattered on the walls and floor going down, indicating that Kane had hit somebody when he shot back (although she didn't see any bodies). They wouldn't be able to make it down without stepping in it, and they weren't eager to leave a trail of bloody footprints that someone could follow

Ultimately, they had taken one of the other stairwells down. Mika hadn't been sure Kane could make it, but he obviously had an iron will because he held it together until they reached the bottom. They only ran into someone once: at the second floor, an old lady and a couple of kids had unexpectedly opened the stairwell door and stepped inside as Mika and Kane were coming down. Kane had reflexively raised his gun at them. The old lady had looked scared to death, but to her credit she stepped protectively in front of the kids; then, she had slowly backed them all out of the stairwell and closed the door without saying a word.

Eventually, Mika and Kane reached the bottom floor and slipped out one of the back doors. The rear of the tenement was much like the front, except – unlike the night before – Mika really didn't see anyone around. At a guess, she assumed niggas had scattered at the sound of gunshots, which had probably echoed throughout the building. However, that didn't mean there weren't eyes on her and Kane.

"Your car?" she asked.

Kane gestured vaguely, and a moment later he and Mika were headed in that direction, moving as swiftly as possible across frost-covered ground. A few minutes later, they got to his car – a mid-sized import with tinted windows parked about two blocks away.

"This was as close as you could get?" Mika admonished as she propped Kane up against the passenger side of the car. Having borne the bulk of his weight since leaving the apartment, she was slightly out of breath.

"Noose...parked...out front," he mumbled as Mika fished the keys out of his pocket.

Mika nodded in understanding. Kane and Noose had arrived in another vehicle and parked it in front of the projects where the apartment was. This car had been kind of a back-up, in case something went wrong with the other car or they had to abandon it.

Mika had to admit to being impressed; it was more foresight than most niggas showed. Plus, the import was fairly inconspicuous. It wasn't a new model, didn't have fancy wheels, and was actually dinged in a couple of spots.

Once she got the keys out, she opened the passenger door and helped Kane in. Then she hustled around to the driver's side. A moment later, they were in motion – and seemingly just in time, as a black, late-model

70

SUV went streaking by them in the direction of the tenement they'd just left. Looking in the rearview mirror, Mika saw it screech to a halt, and then four niggas who looked like they were on a serious fucking mission went dashing out of it towards the building entrance.

It was all Mika could do not to slam on the gas and burn rubber trying to get away.

Chapter 15

Mika drove randomly for a few minutes, focused mostly on just putting distance between her and the tenement. Kane suddenly moaned, reminding her that he was injured.

"Look, you gotta get some help," she said to him as she cranked up the heat in the car. "We need to get you to the emergency room."

"No," he replied fervently. "Need Doc."

"That's what I'm saying – you need a doctor."

Kane shook his head firmly. "No. Just need…Doc."

"Yes, a doctor, you stupid nigga. That's what I've been saying."

"Not a doctor," he replied. "*Doc.*"

"Huh?" Mika muttered, confused. She didn't know what the hell he was talking about.

An odd motion from Kane drew her attention, and glanced over to see that he had pulled out his cell phone with his free hand (the other still held his gun) and was pressing digits. A moment later, it started ringing. And then Kane's hand flopped loosely onto his chest, and Mika realized he had passed out, still holding the phone.

"Hello?" she heard someone say on the phone in a gruff voice. "Hello?"

"Shit," she muttered, then – gripping the wheel with her left hand – she leaned over and took the phone from Kane's limp hand.

"Hello?" said the voice again as she put it on speakerphone.

"Uh, hello," Mika said. "Can you hear me?"

There was silence for a moment, then the voice demanded, "Who is this?"

"I'm, uh…" she began. "I mean I'm… I'm a friend of Kane. I'm trying to reach Doc."

"Kane?" the voice – presumably Doc – repeated.

"Yeah," she stated. "I'm with him and he's been shot. He started to call you and then he passed out."

"Where?"

"Uh…I'm not sure – somewhere near downtown. I've just been driving around trying to figure out where to go."

"No, genius! Where's he been *shot?*"

"Oh," she muttered. "Ah, the stomach. He's bleeding a lot."

"Really? Bleeding? That's unusual with gunshot wounds," Doc declared acerbically. "Okay, I'm going to give you an address. Think you can find it?"

"I got GPS on my phone."

"So is that a yes or a no?"

"Yeah, I'm sure I can…" Mika began. "I mean, I think… Uh, yeah, I can find it."

"Whatever…" Doc said, not sounding convinced. He then gave her an address before hanging up abruptly.

Chapter 16

The address turned out to be a small farmhouse about an hour outside the city. She half-carried Kane up to the porch and banged on the door, but from all indications, no one was home.

"Key…" Kane muttered, waving at his keyring that she was holding. She had automatically taken it when they'd gotten out of the car and still had it in her hand.

There were a number of keys on it, but after a little trial and error she found one that unlocked the door. A moment later, they staggered inside.

The interior was cold and dark; all the windows had blinds which were closed and drapes which were drawn. Mika kicked the door shut and then felt around on a nearby wall until her hand came across a light switch. She turned it on and saw that they were in a cozy living room with a fireplace.

"Come on," she said, starting to guide Kane to a nearby couch. Her breath frosted as she spoke, indicating that it was probably as cold inside as outdoors.

"No," Kane said, then pointed towards the kitchen. "The table."

Mika frowned in confusion. "Huh?"

"He's gonna want me on the table," Kane replied, as if that explained everything.

Still unsure, Mika helped him into the kitchen where she saw a wooden, rectangular breakfast table. It was covered with a cheesy, red-and-white checkered tablecloth made of plastic and had six chairs around it: one on each end and two on each side.

Following Kane's lead, Mika helped him over to the table. Then, showing more strength than she'd thought

74

him capable of, he stood up straight and shrugged, groaning audibly as he tried to get his coat off. Once she realize what he was trying to do, Mika helped slip the coat from his shoulders and pulled it off as gently as she could. Then, without prompting, Kane flopped onto the table, stretching out lengthwise. Seconds later, he was knocked out – having either fallen asleep or passed out.

Chapter 17

They had been at the farmhouse maybe thirty minutes when Mika heard a vehicle pull up outside. Gun in hand, she peeked out the blinds and she saw a car in the driveway parked next to Kane's vehicle. A man got out wearing a trench coat and carrying a black doctor's bag.

He was bald and clean-shaven, which made it difficult to guess his age, but - based on some lines in his dark-complexioned face – Mika pegged him at about sixty or so. That said, he was kind of spry in the way he moved, not giving the impression of being old or infirm. He stepped up on the porch and knocked on the door.

Still holding the gun, she stepped to the door and then, with her back to the wall by the door frame, shouted, "Who is it?"

"Doc," answered the man outside. "Open the damn door – it's cold out here."

Mika debated for a moment, then tucked the gun back into her sweats, pulled the shirt over it, and opened the door. Doc came in and she immediately shut the door behind him, not wanting to let the warm air out. (She'd found the thermostat after getting Kane settled, and the place was only just getting to a comfortable temperature.)

"A'ight," Doc said. "Where is he?"

"The kitchen," Mika replied, and was about to lead the way when Doc simply turned and went in the right direction. Obviously he'd been there before, which begged the question: how often did Kane get shot?

"Great," Doc said, "he's already on the table."

He placed his bag on the table near Kane's head, then took off his coat and tossed it over the back of one of the chairs.

"Hit that light for me over there, will you, please?" Doc asked, pointing towards the wall.

Mika did as asked, and a hanging lamp positioned over the table blazed to life.

"That's better," Doc declared, then turned his attention to Kane.

He really hadn't moved since Mika had helped him onto the table. Because the room had initially been cold, she'd laid his coat on top of him. (Plus, it seemed like in the movies they were always trying to keep injured people warm.) Looking at him now, she could almost have sworn he was asleep, except he looked incredibly pale.

Doc opened up his bag and pulled out a small flashlight.

"Hey, Sleeping Beauty," Doc muttered as he shined the flashlight into Kane's eyes. "You still with us?"

Kane moaned softly in response.

"I'll take that as a 'Yes,'" Doc said as he put the flashlight aside.

"From what I can see in his eyes, he ain't high," Doc explained to Mika. "But I need to ask you, did he take anything?"

She shook her head. "Not that I'm aware of."

"Good," Doc remarked. He then took the coat off Kane and tossed it to the side.

Reaching into his bag, he pulled out a pair of odd-looking scissors. To Mika, it looked like the blades had been bent in the middle.

"What are those?" she asked.

"Medical shears," Doc replied, and then began using them to cut away the turtleneck, starting at the center near Kane's waist. He then did the same with the t-shirt underneath.

77

"Is that necessary – slicin' his clothes off like that?"

"Naw," Doc said. "I just like cuttin' shit."

Mika let out something like an exasperated sigh, which caused Doc to give her an appraising glance.

"Look, I'm sorry," he apologized. "I'm old and cantankerous, and I've lost patience with people over the years. It's nuthin' personal."

"It's fine," Mika assured him.

"The medical shears are for cuttin' away clothing mostly," he explained, "but can be used on lots of other shit. They can help you get at wounds without havin' to move the injured person around too much."

"I can understand that," she said.

Nodding in response, Doc turned back to his patient.

"What the hell is this?" he asked, indicating the towel that Mika had wrapped around Kane's wound.

"It's a towel," she stated matter-of-factly.

"I can see that, but it looks dirty."

"It's not. I only used it to dry off the last time I took a shower."

"So you dried off with this and then used it on his wound?" Doc asked, looking nonplussed. "Did you at least sterilize it first?"

"Huh?"

"Did you *sterilize* it – pour alcohol or something on it to kill germs and shit?"

"Uh, no."

"Well did you at least put something on the injury to fight infection?"

"No," Mika droned, feeling somewhat ashamed.

"What the fuck?" Doc uttered, sounding flabbergasted.

"Hey, they never do any of that stuff in the movies or on TV," she shot back defensively. "They just wrap those muthafuckas in gauze and boom – they good as new."

"Fuckin' movies and television…" Doc muttered as he unwrapped the towel. "I tell you, the misinformation on those two done killed mo' niggas than the Klan and cancer combined."

Mika lowered her eyes. Noticing this, Doc let out a remorseful sigh.

"Hey," Doc said, "I know you did your best. Let's just focus now on getting' this nigga to pull through."

Chapter 18

It took Doc a few hours to do everything he needed to for Kane: blood transfusion, digging out the bullet, sewing him up, etcetera. He also got a sponge bath (although that was mostly left to Mika since Doc firmly declared, "I ain't washin' that nigga's dick.") Afterwards, they got him into bed in what appeared to be the master bedroom.

As he packed up his bag in the kitchen, Mika had to admit to Doc that she'd been impressed by his work.

"So where'd you go to med school?" she asked.

Doc chuckled. "Army Medical Corps."

"Huh?"

"I was a field medic in 'Nam," he explained.

"Vietnam? Wasn't that like forty years ago?"

"Fifty," Doc corrected. "Nice to know they still teach history in school."

Ignoring the jibe, Mika asked, "So is that where you learned to save people?"

"I ain't learn to save nobody," he clarified. "I just learned how to patch niggas up so that they'd live long enough to reach a real doctor who *could* save 'em."

"Well, it looks like you did fine to me."

A faraway look came into Doc's eyes. "Somewhere along the way, I guess I got good at it. But that just shows how fucked up things were in 'Nam, 'cause it means I had a lotta muhfuckas to practice on."

Unsure of how to respond to that, Mika just stayed silent.

"Anyway," Doc went on, changing the subject, "I gave Kane a local anesthetic for the pain. Basically, he ain't gonna feel much of anything in the area of the wound, but that don't mean he can act as normal. He'll try to, 'cause the nigga's got a high tolerance for pain and will act like nuthin's wrong, but it's a bad idea. He still got trauma there, and if he's not careful he gone aggravate the wound, tear his stitches, or some shit like that."

"So he just need to take it easy."

"Right," Doc agreed with a nod. He then placed three needles filled with fluid on the kitchen counter. "These are three more shots of the anesthetic. Kane knows how to use them, but tell him to take just one every twenty-four hours or it'll fuck him up good."

"Got it," Mika said.

"And you remember how to change the dressing and the other stuff I showed you?"

"Yep," she assured him, reflecting on how, during the past few hours, Doc had given her a crash course in nursing and medical care.

"Good," Doc said. "Now I'm outta here."

Chapter 19

After Doc's departure, Mika scrambled around in the kitchen looking for something to eat. The fridge had drinks stocked (soda, beer, water, etc.), but no food. But that wasn't completely surprising. She'd done a quick tour before Doc arrived – noting that the place was a three-bed, one bath – and it had quickly become evident that nobody lived here. Or rather, nobody lived here on the regular; it seemed more like a caretaker came by every once in a while to make sure the lights still worked and stuff like that.

Ultimately, she found a nice supply of canned goods and prepackaged food in the pantry: soup, veggies, protein bars, etc. There were also some TV dinners, chicken nuggets, and similar items in the freezer.

She put on two cans of soup in a pot she found in the kitchen, and took about half when it was ready. (Thankfully, there were clean dishes and utensils in the cabinets and drawers.) She then curled up on the living room sofa, expecting to watch a movie or something on a television that was mounted over the fireplace.

As it turned out, the fuckin' farmhouse didn't have cable, so all she could pick up were boring-ass local channels. Turning the TV off, she pecked around and found a couple of celebrity magazines on the living room coffee table. Flipping through them was almost as entertaining as watching TV, and kept her preoccupied as she ate.

After finishing the soup, she set the bowl on the coffee table and continued looking at the magazines. Honestly, it had been a long time since she'd read anything (or rather, anything that wasn't on her phone), so it was a pleasant diversion. Nevertheless, despite genuine interest in what she was looking at, she found herself yawning more than once. Telling herself she'd go lie down after finishing the current article she was on, she continued trying to read, but suddenly her eyelids started feeling heavier and heavier…

SHE'S HIS DRUG, HE'S HER THUG

Chapter 20

Mika woke to an odd sound, like a cardboard box being dragged across a tile floor. She glanced around in bewilderment, trying to figure out where the fuck she was for the second time that day, and then it all came to her.

Looking around, she saw Kane leaning against the wall in the hallway that led to the bedrooms. He was barefoot and shirtless, wearing only a pair of boxers. (Doc had cut off his pants to check for additional wounds.) Other than that, the only type of covering he had was a layer of gauze wrapped around his midsection.

Eyeing him from head to toe, Mika couldn't stop the thought that instantly came to mind – *Damn, that nigga fine!* – and then immediately felt guilty about it. The man had been shot, and here she was thinking about how she'd like to fuck his brains out.

Kane straightened up and took a step forward, at which point Mika realized that the sound she'd heard was his feet dragging on the floor as he shuffled forward.

"Hey," she said, jumping up and moving towards him. "You're not supposed to be up."

"What, you a doctor now?" he joked. "I was just seein' how bad I was hurt."

"You say that like *you* a doctor," she shot back. "Come on, let's get you back into bed." As she spoke, she draped one of his arms around her shoulders and wrapped her own arm around him. His body felt like solid muscle, and again she had to turn her mind away from dirty thoughts.

"So, you did this?" he asked, indicating the gauze.

"Naw, that was Doc," Mika replied.

"Doc? I don't even remember talkin' to him."

"That's 'cause you didn't," she explained. "*I* did."

She then gave him a quick rundown of what had happened after Doc arrived. By the time she finished, they were back in the bedroom and she was helping him into bed.

"You hungry?" she asked after he was lying down once more.

"I could stand to eat," Kane answered, "assumin' it all don't come gushin' out this hole in my stomach."

Mika laughed. "I made some soup earlier. Give me a minute and I'll bring you some."

"Sounds like a plan," he said, stretching out and closing his eyes.

Presumably he dozed off, because when he opened his eyes after what felt like a second, there was a bowl of soup on the nightstand next to the bed and Mika propping pillows up behind him to help him sit up. She then sat on the bed next to him and grabbed the bowl of soup. She lifted out a spoonful and pursed her lips, blowing on it gently (which for some reason Kane found incredibly arousing, gutshot or not). She then carefully brought it to his lips, and gently inserted the spoon when he opened his mouth.

"So," he droned as she spooned more of the soup, "this is what it took?"

Mika frowned. "Huh? Whachu talkin' 'bout?"

Kane smiled. "It took me gettin' shot for you to have sommin' to eat with me."

A moment later, they both started laughing.

SHE'S HIS DRUG, HE'S HER THUG

Chapter 21

They spent the next half-hour talking – initially while Mika fed Kane the soup, and continuing after the food was all gone. As to subject matter, the conversation jumped around haphazardly, with them discussing everything from movies to politics to education.

For Mika, it felt like it was the first time she'd had an extended conversation with a man outside her family who wasn't just trying to get in her pants (or, she admitted, vice-versa). More to the point, she felt herself connecting with Kane in a way that she hadn't with guys before.

Oddly enough, despite going through a good number of topics, the one thing they *didn't* discuss was their current predicament. (Basically, Mika got the sense that Kane didn't want to talk about it.) The closest they came was Mika asking for more info about Doc.

"He's a friend of the family," Kane explained. "He served with my granddaddy in Vietnam."

That had seemed to be about as much as Kane wanted to say about it. In addition, he had punctuated the statement with a yawn, giving Mika the impression he was tired. Thus, she grabbed the bowl and left.

Once in the kitchen, she spent a few minutes washing up both his bowl and hers, as well as their utensils. After laying them in a nearby dish rack, she slipped quietly back down the hall and peeked in on Kane. He appeared to be asleep, so Mika gently closed the door.

She went back to the kitchen and got a bottle of water from the refrigerator. As she twisted off the cap and took a drink, she noticed Kane's coat lying on the floor where Doc had tossed. Setting the water on the counter, she picked up the jacket and spent a moment trying to figure out what to do with it.

Doc had taken the clothes he'd cut off Kane and wrapped them up in the checkered tablecloth that had been on the table. He had then found a garbage bag under the kitchen sink, tossed everything inside, and tied it up.

Presumably, the cut-up clothes could be thrown away, and Mika was wondering if she should do the same with the coat. In the end, however, she took it to the bathroom and spent fifteen minutes scrubbing it with a towel she got from a nearby linen closet, trying to remove any bloodstains. When she was done, she felt the coat would pass any visual test, but – based on what she'd seen on cops shows – police could probably figure out that there had been blood on it. (Of course, it had been Kane's blood on the coat, so unless he turned up dead it was probably a non-issue.) Still holding the coat, she went into one of the two empty bedrooms and hung it up in a closet.

At that juncture, having just scrubbed a bloody coat clean, Mika felt she needed a shower. Since she didn't have any of her own things with her, she rummaged through the closets and dressers of the two empty bedrooms until she found something suitable: an over-sized men's t-shirt. It wasn't perfect, but it would serve.

Taking the t-shirt with her, she went back to the bathroom, stripped, and then took a long, leisurely shower (during which she tried not to think about all the shit that had happened throughout the day.) When she got out, Mika debated putting her bra and panties back on, but suddenly realized that they were the only underwear she currently had. She wasn't sure how long she'd be at this place, but she knew she'd start feeling cruddy if she had to wear the same, unwashed underwear two days in a row.

(Even when she'd been on the run, she'd sometimes wear the same clothes several days in a row, but she always had on clean underwear – even if she had to wash the same ones every night by hand.)

Ultimately, she ended up just slipping on the t-shirt with nothing on underneath. Earlier, she'd come across a washer and dryer in a small utility room at the back of the house, so she gathered up her things, went there, and put her clothes in the washer. It was an older model, but coming from the hood, it wasn't anything she hadn't seen before. Thus, a minute later, she had the washer started.

Having finally reached a point where she could take a break, Mika spent a moment checking her cell phone. She had turned it off during the drive from the city to the farm, and only switched it on long enough to see that there were a million calls and texts from Nay-Nay's dumb ass. No way was she returning those – at least not right now, not from *her* phone.

During the months that she'd been gone, she had disconnected all location services from her phone. It was at that point that she'd realized just how many fuckin' apps and shit are all up in your business: "So-and-so app would like to access your location. Allow?"

Fuck naw, nigga! was her automatic response these days, although there had been a time when she hadn't paid attention. During her time on the road, though, she'd not only become wise to that shit, she'd practically become a fuckin' expert on shit like triangulating location based on cell towers. Again, she didn't think niggas in the hood were up on that shit, but she had made it her business to learn about it because she hadn't known who might have been after her.

SHE'S HIS DRUG, HE'S HER THUG

At that point, Mika's thoughts naturally turned to Kane. She assumed he was still sleeping, but decided to go check on him. As she suspected, he was still knocked out. However, laying on the nightstand next to the bed was his gun.

Mika frowned. After she'd gotten him inside, she hadn't really known what to do with the gun. Ultimately, she had placed it – along with his other possessions (wallet, keys, etcetera) – in the nightstand drawer, although not before sneaking a peek at his license and seeing that his age was twenty-two. Like a lot of niggas, Kane apparently needed to have a weapon on hand in order to sleep easily, and had poked around until he'd found it. (By contrast, her own gun was on the dresser in the bedroom where she'd come across the t-shirt.)

Having seen enough movies where a wounded, half-conscious character accidentally shoots somebody, Mika made a decision to put the gun a little further out of reach. She walked to the nightstand and was about to take the weapon when something else drew her attention: on the side away from her, Kane had apparently fallen asleep with a book in his hand. His arm flopped over to the side, he still had a thumb in between the pages, presumably marking the spot where he'd been reading.

Mika, couldn't help but be surprised. Half the niggas she knew could barely read, including ones with diplomas (which just went to show how fucked up the school system was in the inner city). On top of that, most of them muthafuckas acted like books were an STD – like you'd pick up something contagious if you touched one. Kane obviously had no such compunctions.

There was a bookcase in the bedroom, but Mika had barely noticed it – or rather, the fact that it actually had books on it. Most bookcases she'd seen in the projects were typically used for something else: holding plants, pictures, or some shit like that... Maybe some high school *year*books, but not regular books. Presumably Kane had gotten the title in his hand from the bookcase, and it begged the question: What does a drug-dealing, gangsta nigga read?

The question alone was deep and profound. It was the kind of philosophical shit that white grad students wrote papers on (or discussed with their contemporaries while passing around a joint and listening to Tupac).

Curious now, Mika leaned across Kane's chest, placing a hand on the other side of the bed to steady herself. She was just making out the title – something about a biography, and that's when it happened.

Apparently, Mika hadn't paid attention to just how close she was to Kane's head. (Or maybe when she placed her hand on the other side of him for balance, the bed had given more than she'd anticipated.) Regardless, her left breast brushed up against his face – his lips to be precise – just as he exhaled deeply.

She felt his breath through the thin t-shirt, a small gust of warm, soothing air that hit her areola and spread across her nipple like wildfire. It caught her so by surprise that she let out a small gasp and froze, feeling her nipple harden like it had turned to concrete.

Was this where she was now? Was she actually that horny? Had she gone so long without a dick inside her that this was all it took – a man simply breathing in her fucking direction – to get her excited?

Strengthening her resolve, she slowly began straightening up. As her face passed Kane's, she glanced in his direction and got a shock: he was awake.

Their eyes locked and she stopped moving – just stayed there, staring at him. It was as if she were a bird that had been mesmerized by a snake. There was something in his eyes...something strong, powerful, and compelling. Something that moved her on a deep-rooted, emotional level. She was so entranced that she didn't even notice when he placed his hand behind her head, then gently – but firmly – pulled her mouth towards his until their lips touched.

The kiss was electrifying – an expression of overwhelming want and unconscious desire. It filled some need in her but at the same time, left her hungry for more, and was so unexpectedly intense and impassioned that it overrode conscious thought.

When she finally was able to think straight again a minute or so later, she realized that at some point during their kiss she had straddled him. Moreover, she was unconsciously, rhythmically arching and relaxing her back every few seconds, sliding her pussy up and down the length of his dick, which was still in his boxers but now like a rod of steel.

Breathless, she pulled away slightly, placing her cheek next to his.

"We can't," she muttered. "You still hurt."

"Doc numbed the area," Kane replied. "I can't feel nothing."

"We'll tear the stitches," she shot back, realizing that despite her objections, her pussy was still stroking his dick.

And soaking his boxers, she thought. At the same time, she notice that he'd slipped a hand under the t-shirt and was fondling her nipples and tits in a way that was starting to make her head spin.

While she still had her thoughts together (and a little intestinal fortitude), Mika forced herself to sit up straight. She was preparing to slide off him when a firm hand suddenly grabbed her ass.

"Where you thank you goin'?" he almost hissed. "Bring that pussy here."

Both hands gripping her ass now, he tugged her towards his face, and Mika found herself willingly sliding forward. A moment later his mouth was at her pussy, and Mika moaned unexpectedly and loudly, at the same time closing her eyes.

He went to town then – licking, sucking, nibbling gently… Every stroke of his tongue made her shiver, every touch of his lips made her shake. Having his mouth on her was intoxicating, like a drug she couldn't get enough of. And then he discovered her clit.

"Oh, shit!" she shouted when he first put his tongue on it. At that moment, she understood somewhere in the back of her mind that everything he'd been doing with his mouth up until then – playing in the area around her clit with his tongue, lips and teeth – was just the appetizer. Now it was time for the main course.

She practically screamed nonstop after that as Kane took control of her via her clit. He circled it teasingly with his mouth, licked it lovingly, rolled his tongue around it like a blanket… That and what felt like a thousand other things that set her body on fire.

Mika found herself thrusting against him involuntarily, damn near trying to swallow his head with her snatch. At the same time, she leaned forward, gripping the bed's wooden headboard like she was trying to break that muthafucka in two. If it was intoxicating before, it was a fucking out-of-body experience now as his mouth took her to new heights and had her shaking like a damn earthquake had hit.

"Oh, fuck!" she cried. "I'm cummin'! I'm cummin'! I'm cummin'!"

Kane didn't ease up. If anything, he licked harder and faster, eliciting more cries out of her before putting his lips on her clit and humming. It made his lips vibrate and sent a kaleidoscope of color and light into Mika's brain that was so intense that it was blinding. It transformed an orgasm that was already explosive into one that was earth-shattering, initiating a shock to the system that made her scream so loud she thought she'd ripped a vocal cord.

Chapter 22

To Mika, it felt like forever before she could move again. In fact, she found that she had clenched her legs together so tightly around Kane's head (and buried his face so deep in her pussy) that she thought she'd smothered that nigga.

Moving like an old woman, she moaned as she slowly backed away from his face, trying to be careful of his wound. When she was once again straddling his hips (and feeling that still-hard dick), she leaned forward and put her mouth near his ear.

"Your turn..." she muttered, then continued sliding down his body until her face was above his groin. At that point she laughed and looked at him.

"You cocky muthafucka," she said with a grin.

"What?" he droned innocently.

"What happened to your boxers?" Mika inquired.

Kane raised his head a little and looked down. "What the...? Where da fuck they go?"

Mika laughed again. Sometime while he was making her cum, Kane had slipped of his boxers – like the nigga just knew he was gonna get *some*thing.

•   "Well, we can't have you gettin' cold," she said, cupping his balls with one hand as she began to work the shaft with the other. "Let's what we can do to warm you up."

Groaning in pleasure, Kane laid his head back down and closed his eyes.

Mika pressed her lips to the tip of his dick, intentionally making a kissing sound. Then she licked it, going up one side and down the other before giving his balls the same treatment.

She continued cupping his balls with one hand, gently giving them an occasional squeeze while with her mouth she played the same teasing game he'd done with her: running her lips all around his dick, continually going to the tip like she was about to suck it, then moving on without doing so.

When she finally did take him in her mouth, Kane felt like he was ready to explode, his dick throbbing relentlessly in anticipation. At that juncture, Mika revealed dick-sucking to be one of her core strengths, as she continually brought him to the brink of cumming but never took him all the way. Within two minutes, he was begging for the pussy.

"Come on," he urged, trying to pull her forward. "I wanna fuck you."

She pushed his hands away, initially – continuing to enjoy the taste of him while also sending the message that *she* was the one running the fucking show at the moment. It wasn't until he relented, surrendering to her, so-to-speak, that she finally took her mouth off him. Then she quickly sat up and straddled him again, then slid her hot, wet pussy down over his engorged dick.

It felt divine as he went inside her, an inner flower spreading out and opening up to the warmth of the sun. At first Mika tried to go gently because of his injury, but within just a few strokes that shit was feeling way too good.

Fuck it, she finally said to herself. *Either he lives or dies. Either way, I'm sending this nigga to heaven to tonight.*

Mind made up, Mika rode his dick mercilessly from that point forward. Putting her hands on his chest, she nimbly and consistently brought her hips up-and-down in rhythmic fashion, taking in the length of him over and over again with single-minded purpose. To his credit, one of his hands found her clit again, thumb rubbing it as she bounced up and down on his pole, while his other hand went to her tits and played with them and her nipples. When she came, it was with three erogenous zones – her g-spot, clit and nipples – all being stimulated, and she damn near started glowing like a hundred-watt bulb, feeling like every nerve in her body was alive and tingling for the first time in her life.

Chapter 23

Bliss, Mika thought as she lay in bed next to Kane. That was the only word that she could think of to describe how she felt after fucking him. *Complete and absolute fucking bliss.*

She knew without asking that Kane felt the same. He had cum with her, and simply lay there after she collapsed next to him on the bed, breathlessly muttering "Damn" and "Holy shit" over and over again.

Mika smiled. There wasn't a whole lot that she could claim to be great it. She was generally an okay employee, a moderately good cook, and so on. But one thing she was absolutely outstanding at was fucking. She ranked world-class in that shit, as this nigga had just learned.

At the same time, however, she had to admit that Kane had game as well. He knew how to get a woman off – in fact, that nigga was fucking gifted in that arena. Mika realized that she had to be careful around this muthafucka, because a bitch could get hooked on that shit.

And speaking of being careful around him, it finally seemed to her that it was time to have the conversation she needed to with him.

So, after a quick trip to the bathroom to get cleaned up (part of her post-fucking routine), she got back in bed beside him. Turning on her side, she stared at him for a few seconds, then asked, "Why?"

Kane turned his head in her direction. "Why what?"

"When you found me in that closet, why'd you let me go?"

He didn't immediately answer. Instead, he turned his face back towards the ceiling and merely looked up, staring so intently that anyone watching would have thought he had x-ray vision and was looking through the ceiling at something else.

The silence felt extended, but was probably no more than fifteen seconds, and then he spoke.

"It's because of my sister," he finally said.

"Your sister?" she repeated, frowning in confusion.

Kane nodded. "She got caught up with some nigga – a wannabe gangsta who she thought loved her 'cause he occasionally bought her some cheap shit, like two-dollar earrings from a pawn shop. Anyway, he crossed the wrong muhfucka – an asshole named Jamil, who decided he wanted a pound of flesh as payback. So he and his boys broke into the boyfriend's place one night and shot him. And my sister happened to be there."

Mika merely stared at him, seeing that this was disturbing for Kane. After a moment, she asked, "What happened?"

"They shot her. Killed her."

"Oh," Mika uttered somberly. "I'm so sorry."

As she spoke, she reached out and gently and took his hand, giving it a comforting squeeze. Some niggas might have moved their hand away at that point just to show they were all hard and shit, but not Kane. Apparently he had nothing to prove, because he gripped her hand back.

"They didn't have to do it – shoot her, that is. I mean, it's the hood. Muhfuckas do driveby's in broad daylight and don't care who sees them. But Jamil was a sadistic piece-a-shit, and my sister was at the wrong place at the wrong time."

"That's terrible," Mika said in sympathy.

"You wanna know the worse part? That muhfucka Jamil was out there bragging about killing her boyfriend less than a day later. If he was gonna be tellin' everybody about that shit hisself, why'd he have to shoot my sister? She was only fifteen."

"Fifteen?" Mika echoed incredulously.

"Yeah. And the muhfucka she was foolin' with was damn near ten years older than her. Fuckin' pedophile... Anyway, when I saw you in that closet, it was like my sister – wrong place, wrong time. So I thought it best to just let you go."

"After scarin' the shit outta me by takin' my license."

Kane chuckled. "Yeah, I had to do something to make sure you stayed in line. I tried to return it and explain that you ain't have nuthin' to worry about, but you were ghost at that point."

"Muthafucka, what did you think I was gonna do?" she said angrily. "Wait for you to show up and blow my brains out?"

He laughed. "I like the way you say that."

"Say what?"

"Mu-tha-fuck-a," he said, stressing each part of the word. "You say it all fancy, with fo' syllables. Most niggas just say 'muhfucka' – with three."

"What can I say? I'm a classy fuckin' lady, nigga."

He chortled at that, and she joined him a second later.

"Seriously though," she continued, "that's just how my family says it. I think somebody mentioned it before, but it's not like grammar is a strong point for niggas in the projects."

"No argument there."

Mika was silent for a moment, then asked, "So what happened to the guy who shot your sister?"

Kane frowned. "Justice happened to his black ass."

"What does that mean?"

"Jamil got what he deserved. But to be honest, if he hadn't said anything about it, hadn't been bragging about it, I... I probably wouldn't have done it."

Mika gave him a confused look. "Done what?"

Kane glanced in her direction. "I shot him."

"What?"

"Yeah. Gettin' a piece was no big thang – everybody's got a gun, and for the right price you can pick one up cheap. I got one of my boys to sell me one. Then I just went to this chicken spot Jamil would go by at least once a day and waited."

"Did he show up?"

"Oh yeah, him and a couple of his boys pulled up in a big SUV. He liked to go in himself because the owner gave him free bird whenever he came in – Jamil had it like that at a couple of places. So when he got out and was walking to the door, I stepped forward and shot him in the head. No words, no explanation about why I was there, no making him understand why it was happenin'. I didn't need him to know the why of it. *I* knew. He dropped to the ground, and that was it."

"What about the people with him?"

Kane laughed. "You know, muhfuckas act all hard and shit, flashin' they pieces all the time, but most of them niggas ain't never been in an actual gunfight. That was Jamil's boys. There was like four of 'em, and one of 'em was so nervous he actually dropped his piece while pulling it out. The other three got they guns out, but basically just

100

fired blindly behind them as they ran for cover. In fact, I think two of them niggas shot each other."

"What did you do?"

"I walked away without a scratch on me," he said, grinning at the memory. "But it didn't take'em long to find me. That picked me up that evening and took me to see Deke."

"Deke?" Mika asked in surprise. "You talkin' 'bout Deacon Black?"

Kane nodded. "Yeah. Guess you heard of 'im."

"Hell, everybody heard of Deke. He owned the streets. He was runnin' buddies with my Uncle Zeke back in the day. The 'Deke and Zeke Show' they used to call 'em."

"You mean Zeke Green?" Kane asked in surprised. "The one they used to call 'Mean Green?' That's your uncle?"

"Yeah," Mika answered. "But he's been locked up forever."

"What for?"

"Killing a kid. His own son."

"What da fuck?" Kane blurted out, almost in shock.

"He was high at the time," Mika said, "and was actually aimin' at his baby momma. The boy saw what he was doin' and stepped in front of his momma just as Uncle Zeke pulled the trigger."

"Damn..." Kane muttered. "That's more fucked up than the shit with my sister."

"Anyway, I didn't mean to derail the conversation," Mika stated. "What happened with Deke?"

Kane concentrated for a moment, then said, "Like a bunch of niggas back then, Jamil worked for Deke.

Normally, killing somebody in his organization meant they'd light yo ass up – make an example out of you. But that was when it was about business – when somebody was tryin' to take over his territory or some shit like that. Deke understood that the shit with me had been personal, but he couldn't just have muhfuckas thinkin' it was okay to blow away his employees, so he gave me a choice."

"Which was what?"

"He said that killing Jamil had left a void in his organization, and – as Deke put it – nature abhors a vacuum. So I could fill that void, or fill a grave."

"And you chose the void."

Kane shrugged. "Fillin' a grave wouldn't do anything for anybody except maggots."

Mika frowned. "But what if some of Jamil's buddies came lookin' for revenge?"

"Deke put the word out that Jamil had been stealin' from him, and that it had needed handlin'."

"And people believed that?"

Kane snickered. "According to Deke, everybody steals – most of 'em just do it in small enough amounts that it ain't worth the trouble to get rid of 'em. You just drop hints every now and then that you know what they up to, and they'll pretty much stay the fuck in line."

"So what did you do for him?"

"I was a lookout at first, then moved up to runner. Most of the time I was paired with my boy Jaycee, who was already working for Deke, so naturally we became partners and moved up the food chain together."

"And now?"

"I guess you could say we're middle management, shootin' for a promotion."

"Funny," Mika remarked. "You don't strike me as the type."

"What, I'm not management material?"

"*Drug dealer* material," she clarified.

"Why you say that?"

"For one thang, you fell asleep with a book in yo hand, and most of those niggas couldn't pick a book out of a lineup in a library. What were you readin' anyway?"

Kane grabbed the book from the nightstand, where he had moved after Mika had climbed off his dick and collapsed onto the bed next to him.

"It's a book of biographies," he said, showing her the cover. "They got a bunch of famous people in here, listed A-to-Z, and I was just reading up on 'em."

"Famous people?" she repeated. "Like movie stars, singers, and people in celebrity magazines?"

"People who're famous in all areas – doctors, lawyers, kings, generals... Anybody who had an impact."

"Sounds interestin'," Mika said, stifling a yawn. "Read me one of 'em."

"Alright, let's start with somebody you might have heard of," he said, flipping through pages. "Genghis Khan..."

Chapter 24

Mika woke up alone in bed, roused by a sound that was both odd and familiar: a peculiar cracking and popping noise that almost sent her into a panic at first.

Fire! she thought. She'd been around enough fires in the hood – in drum barrels, barbecue pits, and (on more than one occasion) in apartments – to recognize the distinct sound of crackling flames. But then her mind put everything into context for her and she relaxed.

She'd fallen asleep to Kane reading to her from the book of biographies. Now, of course, he was gone, but she had a suspicion as to where he was.

Taking the blanket from the bed, she draped it over her shoulders and walked down the hallway to the living room. There, as expected, she saw Kane with a poker, tending to some wood that was burning in the fireplace.

He looked in her direction as she came in. He was dressed in the boxers again, but his physique – bathed in light from the fireplace – was dreamy.

"Hey," he said, giving her a smile that made her heart flutter a little.

"Hey yourself," Mika shot back as she walked over and sat down crossed-legged on the floor next to him.

"Sorry if I woke you," he said. "I only get out to this place every few weeks, and I usually try to make sure everything's still working."

"Includin' the fireplace?" she asked.

"Only in winter," he said with a wink. "It helps keep animals from trying to nest in there, or use it as a way to get in."

"So this is your place – the farm, I mean?"

Kane nodded. "My grandfather bought it years ago, planned on moving the family out here. He wanted us out of the hood, basically."

"So what happened?"

"This place was falling apart when he bought it, and he died before he could get it fixed up."

"So you never lived here?"

"No. Later, after my grandmother died, it passed to me and some cousins. They all moved away with no plans to come back, so I bought them out and then fixed it up somewhat."

"Are you guys close?"

Kane shrugged. "We were all raised by our grandparents, who had high standards. Basically, I was never supposed to be a drug dealer. I was supposed to be a doctor, a lawyer, or some shit like that. But after my deal with Deke, options were limited – for me, anyway."

"So where are they now?"

"One's an officer in the military. Another one's a doctor. Got another who's a stock broker."

"Impressive."

"Yeah, they got out the hood like our grandparents wanted – avoided gettin' caught up in shit like me. We still talk on the regular, but they pretty much keep me out of their lives, and I can't blame 'em."

Looking to change the subject, she stared at the burning wood for a second and then commented, "Nice job on the fire."

"Thanks," he replied sincerely. "I don't get much practice, so the fact that I got it even lit is a minor miracle."

Mika was silent for a moment, absorbing this. Hearing Kane talk about fire and flames brought something to mind, causing her to broach a topic that had been on her mind for months.

"So, what you mentioned earlier about everybody stealin'... Is that what happened to Tweet?" she asked. "He stole sommin'?"

Kane made a vague gesture. "Pretty much."

"Well, when I was hidin' in that closet, you mentioned sommin' 'bout burning his place down."

"Yeah, didn't happen," he admitted. "Mostly, I wanted to get Jaycee out of there. He's my best friend and partner – like a brutha to me – but I didn't know what he'd do if he saw you there. After we left, I told him I had a different idea and hustled back up to the apartment, hoping to catch you and explain, but you were already gone."

"Sorry buddy, I had a bus to catch," she said with a wink. "But I'm curious as to what your idea was."

"We'd planned to hit a strip club later that night, so we had a bunch of singles with us. I took a stack of them and threw about twenty of 'em into the air in Tweet's livin' room and let 'em flutter to the floor. Then I tossed a few in the kitchen, leavin' 'em on the floor and the counter, and then in the bedroom and bathroom. I also left some stickin' out of cabinets throughout the place, and stickin' out from under the pantry door. Then I walked out, leaving the door to Tweet's place open."

Mika could guess the rest. "Niggas came in unbothered by a dead body and scooped up all the cash they could find. In fact, they probably searched the whole dame place, looking for money"

"Not just cash," Kane clarified. "They were looking for anything they could take and stole everything that wasn't nailed down. Then they went out and bragged, causing more muhfuckas to go in there and tear the place apart, looking for shit."

"You musta known that would happen," Mika said, "so what was the point?"

"The point was that too much evidence is worse than too little. When someone finally called the cops after a day or two, they had a ransacked apartment that looked like the focus of a robbery, and a million prints and DNA to sort through."

"So instead of two or three suspects, they had dozens," Mika concluded.

Kane grinned. "Now you get it."

Mika gave him an appraising glance. She had to admit that what he'd done was pretty slick.

"You cold?" he asked, putting his arm around her.

"No," she said, shaking her head. "I'm okay."

"Oh. I thought I saw you shiver."

As he spoke, he gave her shoulder a gentle squeeze and pulled her closer.

"I know what you doin'," she said.

"Huh?" he muttered, looking confused. "Whachu mean?"

"The romantic fireplace. This little arm maneuver, like some nigga yawning and stretching in order to put his arm around a girl in movie. How many bitches you pull this shit on?"

"None," Kane practically swore. "I never do shit like this with bitches. Only hoes…"

"You muthafucka!" Mika blurted out, laughing as she playfully slapped his chest.

Laughing, Kane caught her wrists and pulled her in close. Giggling, Mika looked into his eyes and was inexplicably drawn in. In them, she saw so much: humor, life, want, desire... To her surprise, she suddenly realized that much of it was a reflection of her own emotions, and it made her incredibly conscious of her feelings – her inner yearnings and needs. More importantly, she felt an immediate and overpowering connection with Kane, and wanted to expand it to all levels.

"Fuck me," she said, before she was even aware that she was going to utter the words.

It was both a request and an order, a plea and a command.

Kane obeyed.

****

Sex the second time was more akin to lovemaking. Like before, there was passion and intensity, but not the same urgency and frenzy that had previously possessed them. There was a sweetness to it that had been lacking before, an unselfishness surrender of self that made it more meaningful.

When they were done, Mika felt it was the most satisfying climax she'd ever had, giving her a sense of completeness with her partner she had never experienced before. As they lay in front of the fire, Kane spooned her, wrapping an around her as her peppered her neck with light, feathery kisses that made her smile.

So this is what that means, she said to herself as she began to doze off. *This is basking in the afterglow...*

SHE'S HIS DRUG, HE'S HER THUG

Chapter 25

For the second time in a row, Mika woke up alone instead of with Kane. This time, however, she was on the floor under the blanket. Looking around, she saw her clothes folded in a neat pile on the living room couch. Apparently Kane had dried them and set them out for her.

Sensing that it was early, Mika glanced at her watch and saw that it was a little after two in the morning. Seeing that, she marveled at how quickly the day had gone by: they'd gotten to the farm a little before noon, and Doc had finished doing his thing by early afternoon. She and Kane had fucked that first time in the early evening, and then again at maybe ten or so.

Sounds form the kitchen interrupted her reverie. Draping the blanket over her shoulders, she hurried there and saw Kane standing near the counter fully dressed.

He was wearing black jeans, black shoes, and a black thermal shirt. At the moment he had the shirt rolled up at the waist and was giving himself an injection near his wound with one of the needles Doc had left.

"Should you be doing that?" Mika asked. "Doc said not to take too much of that shit."

"It's cool," he assured her. "I know how Doc operates. It'll be fine."

Mika wasn't sure about that, but didn't say anything.

"You goin' somewhere?" she asked after a few seconds.

"Yeah," he replied. "I gotta find out who the fuck set me up and sort that shit out."

"What — right now? It's like two in the fuckin' mornin'!"

109

"Which means they won't be expectin' me. I been off the grid for most of the day, so they probably think I'm either dead or laid up somewhere."

Mika, stared at him for a second, then stomped from the room. Kane wondered if he should say something to her, but instead finished with the needle and then tossed it in the trash. As he rolled his shirt down, Mika stalked back into the kitchen, fully dressed.

"Okay," she said, "when do we leave?"

"Oh, no," Kane said. "I can't be dragging yo ass behind me while I'm dealing with this shit."

"You tryin' to say I'll slow you down?"

"I'm tryin' to say I don't want you to get hurt," he clarified. "What you thank gone happen when I find these niggas? You think we gone hold hands and sing 'Kumbaya'? Shit's goin' down!"

"Well, what am I supposed to do, just hang out here?"

"Yeah. Nobody knows about this place – not even Jaycee."

"And if something happens to you what the fuck am I supposed to do – hitchhike back to the city? It's fuckin' December, nigga!"

"Mika," he pleaded, "you don't wanna get caught up in this shit."

"Muthafucka, I'm *already* in this shit!" she exclaimed. "And in case you think all I'm good for is mindblowing sex and monster blowjobs, don't forget that I saved yo ass after you got shot."

Kane just stared at her for a moment, then he laughed.

"You really think that was a monster blowjob?" he said, chuckling. "Babe, you got a lot to learn."

"Nigga, please," Mika droned. "I had you so caught up with that blowjob, you woulda shot yo momma if I'd asked you to."

Kane laughed again. "Alright, but it's yo funeral."

"Whatever," Mika said.

Chapter 26

There was a barn out back behind the farmhouse. Mika had glimpsed it through a window earlier, but hadn't given it much thought. However, it turned out that the barn served as a garage, housing a non-descript, midsized SUV with tinted windows. Kane took a few minutes to swap out the cars, leaving the import they'd arrived in parked in the barn while bringing out the SUV. Then, after gathering some things from the house (like the needles Doc had left and extra bandages, all of which they shoved into the glove compartment), they were ready to go.

"So what's this, yo relaxin'-in-the-country car?" Mika asked as they got on the road.

Kane smiled. "Not exactly. This my low-key-nobody-knows-about-this-shit car."

Mika frowned, thinking. "The farm. This car. Seem like you gotta lotta shit nobody knows about."

"This fuckin' biz that we in, a nigga never know when he gone need to go off the grid. You need assets and resources nobody knows about but you."

"So this car…" Mika began, then trailed off.

"Ain't nobody ever seen me behind the wheel of this bitch except the guy who sold it to me. I check it out every time I go out to the farm, make sure it's still in runnin' condition."

"Pretty smart," Mika admitted. "So where we headed?"

"Need to find Noose."

"Noose," Mika repeated. "That guy who showed up with you at my apartment."

Kane nodded. "Yeah. There were two niggas on the stairs shootin' at me. No way Noose coulda got by 'em

112

without bein' seen, but the first shots they fired were at *me*."

Mika reflected on what she'd heard for a moment, then surmised, "You thank Noose was in on it – that he set you up."

"Well, I got another hint, too: people been blowin' up my cell all day, tryin' to figure out where I am, what the fuck's goin' on, and all that shit. But not Noose."

"Wait a minute," Mika interjected. "You been checkin' yo phone? You know people can track that shit, right?"

Kane smiled. "Yeah, but my phone ain't my phone."

"What da fuck that mean?" Mika demanded, giving him a confused look.

"The cell number that niggas have for me is for a particular phone, but all calls and texts to that number are forwarded to *another* cell. So the number that people have for me ain't the phone I carry on me."

"Damn," Mika muttered, not bothering to hide how impressed she was. "That's pretty damn smart."

Kane shrugged. "Anyway, Noose not checkin' up on me is a sign that he didn't expect me to be in a position to answer. So if that nigga ain't dead…"

He trailed off, but Mika finished for the sentence for him, saying, "…then he set you up."

"Right," Kane acknowledged with a nod.

Mika drummed her fingers for a moment, then asked, "What kind of name is 'Noose,' anyway. He get lynched or something?"

"Not quite," Kane answered. "He done spent a lotta time locked up, and over the years, three of his cellmates apparently hung themselves."

Mika stared him. "You fuckin' kiddin', right?"

"Naw, it's da muhfuckin' truth, I swear."

"No way that's a damn coincidence."

"Well, nobody could prove any of 'em *didn't* commit suicide, but somewhere along the way people started callin' him Noose and it stuck."

"And this is the guy you had as backup?"

"Yeah. He's one of those niggas who's prone to violence, which is what you need in this business."

"But if he knows you're still alive and believe he set you up, won't he be lying low?"

"He prolly knows I got shot and thinks I'm dead or dyin', so why lie low? Plus, he's one of those niggas with too much ego to go into hidin' – thinks he's invincible. But regardless, whether he's lyin' low or not, I know exactly where to find his ass."

Chapter 27

They rode the rest of the way back to town saying little else, but it wasn't strained or awkward. It was a comfortable silence, a peaceful calm before the inevitable storm.

Their journey came to an end at a shitty little motel on the outskirts of the city. It was old and pretty rundown, with an antiquated neon sign flashing "Vacancy." It consisted of four squat buildings spread out over about an acre and joined by a decrepit parking lot that was full of cracks and potholes, as well as pooling water. Unsurprisingly, there were only a handful of cars parked there.

"The fuck we doin' *here*?" Mika asked as they pulled into the lot. "This look like the kinda place where they rent rooms by the hour."

"Oh, so you been here before," Kane quipped as he turned off his headlights.

"Fuck you," she said playfully.

"Maybe later," Kane shot back with a smile.

Mika was about to make a smart-aleck reply when the SUV hit a particularly rough area of the lot.

"Shit!" she belted out as they bounced up and down, despite the fact that Kane was driving pretty slow. "This is like a muthafuckin' rolla-coasta!"

"Guess you're not a fan of amusement parks," said Kane as he brought the SUV to a halt and parked. "Anyway, we're here. Just sit tight and I'll–"

"Fuck that," Mika declared. "I'm comin' with yo black ass."

As she spoke, she pulled out her gun and performed a press check, making sure there was a round chambered. Kane looked at her in surprise, plainly impressed.

"Well alright, then," he muttered, turning the key off and pulling out his own weapon. "Just make sure that if you shoot anybody, it ain't me and ain't you."

He then winked at her and grinned.

"You know, I wish you were this funny when we were fucking," Mika said. "Then I woulda got sommin' out of it."

Kane gave her an evil look. "Get da fuck out my car."

Smiling, she opened the door and slipped out, gently closing it behind her as Kane did the same. He then came around to her side.

The wind was whipping wildly, and it was cold as shit. Almost immediately Mika wished that – like Kane – she had some gloves.

Kane leaned close and said, "Last building."

He pointed as he spoke, indicating a structure at the back of the parking lot that held about a dozen rooms. From what Mika could see, only one of them appeared to be occupied, as evidenced by a light that appeared to be on inside, although the drapes were drawn. Kane had parked maybe a hundred feet away, obviously not wanting anyone inside to know that a car had pulled up.

Hunching low, he ran towards the door of the occupied room, with Mika on his heels. He slowed when he got close, tiptoeing up to the door and then appearing to listen closely. Mika followed his lead, actually putting her ear to the door. Over the howl of the wind, she thought she picked up a repetitive grunting noise that she recognized.

Before she could say anything, Kane stood up straight and took a step back, motioning for her to step to the side (which she did). Then, with his gun out and facing the door, he took a quick step forward, lifted a leg, and landed a solid kick on the door right near the lock.

The door flew open and Kane rushed in, with Mika right behind him. At that point, her eyes saw what her ears had informed her of at the door: there was a couple in the room fucking. More specifically, it was Noose and some chick.

There was a bed in the middle of the room and a bathroom area at the back, and that's where they were. There was a counter about six feet long there, along with a sink and a mirror. Both Noose and the girl were naked, with her bent over and gripping the bathroom counter while Noose pounded that ass from behind. He was so caught up in it that he continued thrusting for a second or two after Kane and Mika broke in.

The girl with him screeched and dropped to the floor, cowering, as Kane kicked the door shut. It was some white bitch with a mess of blond hair that was obviously a wig. She was heavily made up, but Mika could tell that underneath she was probably pretty. However, the make-up and hair, combined with a pair of come-fuck-me pumps that she saw in a corner, told Mika al she needed to know about Noose's playmate: prostitute. That said, Mika had to admit that – prostitute or not – the blonde had perfect tits.

Kane kept his gun on Noose, who didn't move but shot a quick glance across the room. Mika followed his gaze to a small desk where – in addition to the clothes he'd worn earlier – a gun lay. It was too far away for him to get to, but showed what Noose was thinking.

Kane looked pointedly at the prostitute, who flinched under his gaze.

"You don't wanna be here," he said to the blonde. "Take your shit and go."

The prostitute looked like she didn't understand at first, but then scrambled to her feet. That's when Mika got a good look at her and her eyes almost popped out of her skull.

The chick had a dick! She was a tranny!

Struck speechless, Mika merely watched as the tranny scooped up her shit in record time and headed to the door, still naked. (In the back of her mind the tranny's flawless tits made sense now: she'd bought them.)

"Hey," Kane said as the blonde came abreast of him, his voice making her stop and gasp in fright. "Now, I'm not gonna have to worry about you barging back in here with an uzi or some shit like that, trying to save your boyfriend, am I?"

The blonde shook her head fiercely. "He's not my boyfriend. He's just a john."

"You fuckin' bitch!" Noose yelled as the tranny fled out the door, closing it behind her.

Mika, still stunned by what she'd seen, gave Kane a look of incredulity.

"Don't be shocked," Kane said. "See, Noose here is a special type of creature. Most niggas who come out of prison gay were turned out by being someone's bitch on the inside and having they booty taken all the time. But Noose got turned out by *getting* too much booty while locked up. He fell in love with that shit. Now the only thing that excites him is the notion of slidin' in and out of some nigga's hairy asshole. Stickin' it to trannies is just a way of trying to convince himself that he's not a fag."

"Fuck you!" Noose belted out. "I ain't no fag!"

"Really?" Kane uttered in a mocking tone. "I bet if we swing by that tranny strip club you visit every week, they'll say different." Noose's mouth fell open in surprise as Kane went on. "Oh yeah, nigga. I know what you do durin' yo down time. I been waitin' on you to say you givin' up all this gangsta shit to be a drag queen in a Vegas show."

The fury showed in Noose's face as he muttered, "Muhfucka, I'm gone kill you."

"Tsk, tsk, tsk," Kane muttered, shaking his head. "Threatening yo boss? See, this is why you didn't get 'Employee of the Month.'"

"Fuck you, nigga," Noose spat out. "I don't work for *you*. Never did!"

"Now we gettin' somewhere," Kane said. "Who you takin' orders from?" Noose merely rolled his eyes, prompting Kane to continue. "Come on, nigga. We both know you ain't smart enough to cross yo fingers, let alone pull off any kinda *double*-cross. You got the brainpower of a fuckin' housefly."

"Nigga, I ain't tellin' you shit!" Noose exclaimed.

"That's fine," Kane said, nodding. "We can do this shit the hard way, but you ain't gone like it. You gone find it hard fucking niggas doggy-style with no kneecaps."

As he spoke, he lowered his gun, pointing it towards Noose's legs.

"I'll try not to hit ya dick," Kane went on, "but from what I can see, I'd need a rifle with a scope to find that muhfucka."

"Alright, alright," Noose blurted out. "I'll tell you."

Noose lowered his head, looking defeated, and placed his hands on his hips.

"Like I said, I never worked for *you*," he began, lowering his hands to his sides. "I really worked for…*this!*"

Faster than seemed possible, Noose reached behind him as he spoke and flicked something in underhand fashion in Kane's direction. It looked like a glass bottle of some sort, like mouthwash, and Noose immediately followed up his throw by charging at Kane, yelling.

It was a good throw, as the bottle hit Kane's gun hand, spoiling his aim. However, Noose never even reached the bed as two slugs unexpectedly slammed into his chest, spinning him and sending him crashing into the wall. Noose slumped down to the floor, wheezing loudly as blood poured from the two bullet wounds.

Mika stood there, slightly stunned. Noose had apparently been so focused on Kane that he'd forgotten about her. In fact, it looked like he hadn't even noticed that she was packing. (Or, if he had, maybe he somehow assumed that a woman would have qualms about pulling the trigger.) He'd learned the hard way that that was a faulty assumption, although Mika – having never shot anyone before – could hardly believe what she'd done.

"Dumb-ass nigga," Kane muttered, putting his gun away. He then stepped to the table where Noose's clothes were. A quick search of them turned up Noose's wallet, keys, cell phone, and a small roll of single bills.

He pocketed the keys and phone, then took a bunch of singles and tossed them into the air, letting them flutter down to the floor. He then took the wallet and, seemingly on a whim, took Noose's piece.

"You good?" he asked Mika, who merely nodded. "Did you touch anything?"

She reflected for a moment, then shook her head. "No."

Kane nodded, then spent a moment looking around until he spotted the ejected shell casings from her gun. He picked them up and shoved them into a pocket.

"Come on," he said, opening the door. "We gotta move, in case someone heard those shots."

They quickly stepped back out into parking lot (and the freezing weather), leaving the door open to the room they'd left. At that point, Kane pulled out Noose's keys. He appeared to press something, and Mika heard a nearby chirp and caught a flash of light with her peripheral vision.

"Over there," Kane said, and began guiding her in the direction the sound had come from. As they walked, Kane flipped through Noose's wallet; he pocketed some cash he found in it, and then threw the wallet aside.

Noticing Mika giving him an odd look, he explained, "The empty wallet will make police think it was a robbery – especially if people ransack Noose's room like they did Tweet's."

She simply nodded. A few moments later they were in front of a white SUV – presumably Noose's car.

It took almost no time to find what they were looking for: the bag Noose had left the apartment with. It was on the floor behind the driver's seat. Kane unzipped it, peeked inside, then zipped it back up again.

"Okay, let's go," he said.

Minutes later, they were back in Kane's car, leaving the motel in their rearview mirror.

Chapter 28

Once again, there was no conversation as they drove. As before, it wasn't awkward, but it was clear to Mika that Kane was thinking furiously about something.

"So," she droned after about fifteen minutes, "what's next on the agenda?"

"I don't know," he admitted. "I'm trying to figure this shit out."

"Figure what out?"

"Why the fuck Noose still had that bag."

Mika frowned. "Whachu mean?"

Kane looked at her as if contemplating something, then seemed to mentally shrug. "The bag's full of coke – about five keys of the pure."

"I figured that much," Mika stated with a nod.

"Well, I wasn't kiddin' earlier when I said Noose had the brainpower of a fly. He was stupid as fuck, and you don't leave five keys with a braindead nigga like that for an extended period of time, 'cause shit will happen. He'll lose it, snort it, or do sommin' else that'll leave you scratchin' yo fuckin' head."

"So whoever he was workin' fo had him hold it. Why?"

Kane shrugged. "Only thing I can think is that there's sommin' wrong with it. That it's dangerous to have for some reason."

"So why were you dealin' with it in the first place?"

"I guess you don't know how this shit works, so let me educate yo young ass," Kane said. "The coke comes into the States from some other country. It goes through the supply chain – suppliers, dealers, and all that shit – until ultimately it hits the streets. Now as it get passed through

122

all those hands, two things happen: the price keep going up, and the blow keep getting cut. So say you start off with one key that's ninety-five percent pure when it comes into the country and sells for maybe ten gees. It gets cut with some other shit so that you end up with two keys that are almost fifty percent pure that sell for twenty thousand each. By the time it gets into the hands of a dealer who's gonna sell it on the street, it may be four keys that are twenty-five percent pure selling for forty thou apiece."

"I know how it works," Mika told him. "That still don't explain how you got involved with it."

"You remember when I mentioned Deke before? Well, he retired about two years ago – had a massive-ass stroke while high as a fuckin' kite on speedball and knee-deep in pussy. Just a little too much action, I guess. Anyway, his lil' kingdom got divvied up by the folks who worked for 'im, includin' me and Jaycee."

"So you two got your own territory."

"Yeah, and we been runnin' that shit proper, expandin' and everythang. Then we got an opportunity to really blow up."

"The five keys," Mika concluded.

"Yeah," Kane admitted. "We got a connect – a supplier who wanted step away from the distribution network for a hot minute. He offered to partner up with us, give us pure blow directly. We cut it and sell it, then split the profits with him fifty-fifty."

"And you agreed."

Kane shrugged. "You cut five keys of pure coke right, you can get twenty keys out of it. That's worth two million on the street – one mill for me and Jaycee after the split. It was too good to pass up."

"And this connect trusted you to give him his share?"

"Sorta. He wanted us to have skin in the game, so we had to come up with two hundred large to buy in. After the connect got that, he arranged the pick-up, which is where you came in."

"If he already had the cash from you and Jaycee, why even bother with a pick-up? He coulda just had that shit delivered."

"The connect is fuckin' paranoid – don't trust any fuckin' body. This is how he wanted it done, with a middle-man, so we went along. Like I said, this was our shot to join the majors."

"Until somebody set yo ass up."

"Pretty much. But again, there's sommin' going on with this coke. Whoever was bossin' Noose wouldn't leave it with that fool unless it was fuckin' radioactive."

"Well, you knew Noose was cornholin' trannies. You gotta have some idea of who was pullin' that nigga strings."

"I do. I checked his phone. He had a ton of calls today from Jaycee."

Chapter 29

It took fifteen minutes of Mika mercilessly talking about it to convince Kane that he needed to see Jaycee. Kane, for the most part, simply refused that the man he considered his brother would set him up.

"Money changes a nigga," Mika reminded him. "And you said it yo-self – y'all were about to become big-time. Maybe he didn't want to share the throne."

"Jaycee's my boy," Kane said, getting angry. "He wouldn't do that."

"Well, we can keep driving around until the wheels come off this muthafucka, with you tryin' to come up with some other explanation, or you can go see his ass."

Eventually, Kane relented, and a short time later they pulled to a stop on a street lined with cars on both sides. Looking around, Mika saw numerous businesses in the area: a corner store, a cleaners, laundromat, and so on. (Of course, with it being about four in the morning on a Sunday, they were all closed.)

"Okay," Kane said, as he put the car in park. "I'm gonna get out and go down there." He pointed down the street, to a spot where a trio of guys were hanging outside and talking.

"What's down that way?" Mika asked.

"Officially, it's a bar. Unofficially, it's a front for me and Jaycee."

"Oh," she muttered.

"Jaycee lives on the top two floors over the bar. Those fools standin' outside work for us and are s'posed to be standin' guard."

"Okay, whachu need me to do?"

"Well, if those niggas shoot me, it means you were right and Jaycee set me up. If I make it inside okay, I want you to pull around back behind the bar. There's two reserved spots there for me and Jaycee. Park in whichever one is open."

"Okay," Mika said. Then, as Kane was opening the car door, she said, "Hey."

When he turned back to look at her, she leaned over and gave him a kiss. It wasn't long and lingering, but it was deep and passionate.

"Don't get killed," she said.

"It's not on my to-do list," he responded with a wink, then got out and began walking towards the bar.

Chapter 30

Kane didn't have any trouble getting into the bar. He gave each of the guys outside some dap, spoke to them briefly, then went inside.

Seeing that, Mika let out a sigh of relief, then put the SUV in gear and drove. A few minutes later, she was pulling into a reserved parking spot behind the bar. Just as she turned off the lights and put the car in park, a rear door to the bar opened and Kane appeared, waving her inside. She pulled the keys from the ignition, jumped out, and dashed to the door.

Once she was inside, Kane closed the door. Looking around, she saw that they were in a narrow, dimly-lit hallway.

"Come on," he said after she was inside. "There's an elevator down this way."

He began walking, and she followed. A few seconds later, they were at the elevator. There was a big nigga standing guard at the elevator door, but Kane ignored him and in short order were inside it, riding up.

The elevator stopped on a floor that Mika found impressive as she stepped out. The area was clean and well-lit, with a sitting area and thick rugs on the floor. There was also art work on the walls. In general, it gave Mika the impression of a waiting room.

There was a door almost directly across from the elevator. It looked to be of constructed of thick wood and set in a solid frame. Kane went over to the door and started pounding on it. He kept at it for what seemed like forever, but was actually no more than a minute, at which point the door was yanked open and they found themselves staring down the barrel of a shotgun.

Mika froze and there was silence for a moment, then Kane demanded, "Nigga, either let us in or use that thing."

The interior of the room beyond the door was dark, and Mika couldn't make out the person who was holding the shotgun. Then the barrel of the weapon shifted aside and a light came on.

"Nigga, where da fuck you been?" said the person holding the gun, whom Mika recognized as Jaycee. "I been trying to reach yo ass forever."

Jaycee stepped back, inviting them in, and they walked inside.

Mika had thought the space in the hallway outside was nice, but the apartment was fucking swank! There was an expansive living room filled with high-end furniture, a fully stocked bar against a side wall, a smart TV she pegged at no less than eighty inches, and more. There was also a set of stairs leading up to a second floor.

"Who dis?" Jaycee asked, gesturing towards Mika.

"A friend," Kane replied. "She had my back after somebody set us up today."

Kane simply stared at his friend, not saying anything else.

"What — you thank it was *me*?" Jaycee asked in surprise. "Nigga, I oughtta shoot yo ass just for thankin' that. All the shit we been through together, and you thank I'ma set you up?"

"Didn't say it was you," Kane shot back. "Just said it was *some*body."

Jaycee let out a snort of disgust. "Where's Noose?"

"Don't know," Kane answered, and Mika had to fight the urge to look in his direction. "While he was takin'

128

the shit to the car, some muhfuckas opened up on me. Haven't seen him or the shit since. You talked to 'im?"

Jaycee shook his head. "Naw, but I been callin' his ass all day just like I been callin' *you*. Thought you two muhfuckas ran off together."

"Now I oughtta shoot *you* for saying *that*," Kane quipped.

The two men simply looked at each other for a moment, and then both started laughing.

"Da fuck goin' on down there?" said a feminine voice from above them.

Mika looked up and saw a woman standing at the second floor railing. She was tall like Mika, light-skinned, with a head full of bouncy, curly hair. She was dressed in what appeared to be an expensive white bathrobe, but the way it filled out suggested that she had a fashion-model figure.

"It's just Kane, baby," Jaycee shouted back to her.

"Kane?" the woman said in surprise, then started walking down the stairs. "It's fo o'clock in the fuckin' mornin'!"

"Nice to see you, too, Jade," Kane said. "This is Mika."

Mika and Jade exchanged greetings, and Mika noticed that the woman had blue-green eyes.

Jade looked her up and down. "You must be special. Normally by this time, Kane woulda put most girls in a cab and sent 'em home."

Kane gave her an evil look and then stated with a sarcastic tone, "Funny."

Jade flipped her middle finger at Kane, which made her boyfriend chuckle.

Ignoring her, Kane turned to Jaycee and announced, "We need to talk."

"So talk," Jade interjected, flopping down on a couch.

Kane merely looked at her, then back at Jaycee.

"Jade's cool – you know that," Jaycee said. "You can talk in front of her."

"And I prefer to know if my man is mixed up in some crazy shit," Jade added.

"Actually, I was hoping you could show Mika where the kitchen and bathroom are," Kane said to her. "She ain't ate yet, and she was saying when we got here that she needed to pee."

Of course, Mika hadn't said anything along those lines. Truth be told, however, she could stand to use the bathroom and was starting to feel a little peckish, but hadn't wanted to complain.

Jade gave Kane a smoldering look.

"Go on," Jaycee said to her. "Try to be a good fuckin' host for once."

His girlfriend shot an angry glance his way as well, then got up in a huff.

"Come on," she groused as she stomped past Mika, who reluctantly turned and followed her.

Kane watched them walk away for a second, then turned back to Jaycee.

"Don't fuckin' say it," Jaycee practically ordered.

"Say what?" asked Kane.

"The same shit you always say at times like this. That Jade's got me strung out behind her magic pussy."

"Niggas lose they mind behind pussy all the time. That ain't no thang. But you want a girl who's always gonna have yo back. Jade seem like she's just along for the ride.

As long as everything's good and you bathing her ass in caviar and new cars, she by yo side. But the minute shit gets rough she gonna go ghost on yo ass, looking for the next nigga with big bank."

Jaycee shook his head. "Naw, man. You don't know her. She's ride or die."

"Yeah – long as she ain't the one who die."

"Whatever, man," Jaycee said dismissively. "Now let's talk about this other shit."

"I ain't got shit else to say," Kane explained. "We got set up, Noose and the shit are missing, and I spent all day layin' low. What's our connect sayin'?"

"Who, Mo? He the first muhfucka I reached out to when I couldn't get you or Noose. He say we tryin' to rip 'im off."

"What, by stagin' a fake robbery and shootout with real fuckin' bullets? What kinda sense that make?"

"Look, man, I'm just tellin' you what the nigga sayin'."

"Well, what he really sayin' is that only three of us knew exactly what the deal was. Now if *I* was the one pullin' a double-cross, I wouldn't fuckin' be here right now."

"Unless you and Noose really were tryin' to pull a fast one, and then he pulled a Houdini on yo ass and disappeared with the shit."

Kane gave him a stern look. "What da fuck is it with you constantly tryin' to tie me and Noose together?"

Jaycee laughed. "Chill, nigga. I'm just fuckin' with ya. But there is another party that coulda pulled some shit."

"Who?" Kane asked, openly curious.

"The middle-man. The ones Mo used to hold the shit and then hand it off to us."

Kane shook his head. "Naw. I thought about that, but it don't make sense. I mean, they were on site and gave me and Noose the shit. If it was the middle-man settin' us up, why go through all that? They could just plant a bomb or something in the package – rig the box to blow when we opened it up. In fact, they didn't even have to fuckin' be there."

"So what you sayin' is, it's either me or Mo who tried to fuck you."

"Ain't too many other options."

"Well, if it was me, I woulda cut yo ass in two at the door with the shotgun."

"Except then you wouldn't have the blow."

"Well, you say you ain't got it anyway."

"But you didn't know that when you opened the door," Kane reminded him.

Jaycee let out an exhausted sigh. "Alright nigga, I see there's no convincin' yo black ass with words. So how you wanna handle this?"

Before Kane could respond, Jade and Mika returned, with Mika eating an oversized blueberry muffin.

"What we miss?" asked Jade.

"Nothing much," Jaycee said. "Just my partner, best friend, and brutha-from-anutha-mutha accusin' me of settin' him up."

"Naw," Kane declared, shakin' his head. "I said *some*body set me up. It's just that the candidate pool is pretty fuckin' small."

"Fine, then," Jaycee asserted. "Let's go see Mo."

"Naw," Kane stressed, shaking his head. "I need to take care of this shit myself."

"Whatever, nigga," Jaycee huffed. "Anything else I can do for you?"

"No, but I gotta question," Kane stated. "Where do you think he got the keys?"

Jaycee frowned. "Who, Mo? How da fuck should I know? Whoever his usual contact is, I guess. Why?"

"Just tryin' to figure out who else might have an interest in this shit," Kane explained. "Anyway, I'll start with Mo and see what he has to say."

Jaycee nodded in understanding. "You know where to find him?"

"He's a paranoid muhfucka," Kane commented, "but I know where he's holed up."

"Alright," Jaycee said. "You wanna take somma da boys wichu?"

Kane shook his head. "Naw, I got this."

Chapter 31

Mika and Kane left Jaycee's place shortly thereafter, only waiting long enough for Kane to take a bathroom break and grab an apple and banana from the kitchen. Once back in the SUV, they quickly got on the road.

"So, we goin' to see this Mo guy?" Mika asked.

"Yeah," Kane said. "He's our connect – the nigga who came through with the five keys."

"I thought Jaycee was your boy. Why'd you lie to him about not having the coke and not knowing where Noose was?"

"To see what he'd do. If he's working with Noose and he believes Noose has the shit, then what's he need me for?"

"Wait a minute," Mika muttered. "You went up in that muthafucka, knowin' there was a possibility that he might shoot yo ass?"

"Well, there's a possibility that a muhfuckin' jet engine could fall out of the sky and crush the shit out of us right now. It's *pos*sible, but not *pro*bable. Those are two different things."

"What, you a fuckin' professa now? If he'd shoot *yo* ass – his literal fuckin' partner in crime – then he damn sho woulda shot *me*."

"Then I guess it's a damn good thang he didn't."

Mika gave him a hard look. "Next time, I'll wait in the fuckin' car."

"Fine by me."

Mika crossed her arms angrily. "Anyway, where does this Mo asshole live?"

"Apartment complex on the other side of town. He's too paranoid to live in the hood – always thinks someone's watchin' him, plotting sommin'. Don't help that he's always fucking high as well."

"Alright, wake me when we get there," Mika said. She then closed her eyes and lowered her head.

Chapter 32

"We're here," Kane said, placing a hand on Mika's shoulder and shaking her awake.

"Hmm?" Mika droned, coming awake with a start. Seeing Kane, she suddenly remembered where she was and then stretched in an effort to come fully awake.

Looking around, she saw that they were in some kind of parking structure – underground if she wasn't mistaken. They were currently parked in what was marked as a visitor's spot, not too far from an elevator and a stairwell.

"Where are we?" she asked.

"Underground parking garage," Kane replied, then added, "for Mo's building."

"So what now?"

"Now I go upstairs and pay his ass a visit, and try to…"

He trailed off, staring. Mika followed his gaze and saw a man wearing a jogging suit coming out of the stairwell. He had a dark-brown complexion, and was about medium height with a medium build. She pegged his age at mid- to late thirties.

"What is it?" she asked.

"That's that muhfucka right there," Kane answered, indicating the man. "Where da fuck he goin' this early on a Sunday?"

"Morning mass?" Mika suggested as Mo got into an expensive-looking car.

"Only if they do lines after Communion," Kane remarked.

A moment later, Mo started his car and began heading towards the garage exit. Almost immediately afterwards, Kane started the SUV and began following him.

Chapter 33

"This isn't good," Kane said as he drove, staying about half a block behind Mo.

Mika frowned. "Whachu talkin' 'bout?"

"Not enough cars on the street," he explained. "It's still dark out so I doubt that he can really make us out, but like I keep sayin', Mo's a paranoid sumbitch. Sooner or later, he gone notice a pair of headlights constantly in his rearview mirror."

"So kill the lights," Mika said.

"That's just an invitation for the cops to stop you, and do you really wanna get pulled over with what we got in this car?" Kane barked. "The coke. The guns. The keys and cell of some nigga shot dead in a motel room buck naked, with shit all over his dick?"

"Just do it," she ordered. "I'll handle the cops if it comes to that."

Kane looked unsure for a second, then did as suggested and turned his headlights off.

****

Fortunately, they didn't come across any cops, and Mo seemed oblivious to their presence as they drove. Ultimately, they ended up in the warehouse district, where Mo parked outside a large, antiquated building on the right-hand side of the street. It was made of metal and – under the light of a nearby streetlamp – appeared to be rusting in various spots.

Coming to a stop about a block away, Mika and Kane watched as Mo pulled a set of keys from his pocket, then unlocked the door of the building and went inside.

Kane took out his gun and did a press check. Then, after contemplating a moment (and realizing he didn't know how many niggas he might end up facing), he took Noose's gun as well, sticking it in a pocket.

"Okay, I'm gonna go talk to this nigga," Kane said as he put the car in park. "You get yo wish and get to stay in the car this time."

Mika was about to protest, but Kane was already out the car and creeping furtively to the warehouse. She watched him ease the door open and then slip inside.

Chapter 34

The interior of the warehouse was dim. Kane waited a moment, giving his eyes time to adjust to the dark. From what he could make out, the warehouse seemed to be full of cars. However, as his vision adapted, he saw that the vehicles all seemed to be missing various components: doors, a hood, the chassis...

Chop shop, he said to himself as the warehouse's purpose became apparent.

Towards the rear of the building, he saw light in the shape of a rectangle, outlining a door. He swiftly headed for it, then listened for a moment. Not hearing anything on the other side, he opened the door and found himself in a long, narrow hallway.

Stepping quickly but quietly, he strode down the hallway, passing a couple of empty rooms in the process. At the end of the hallway he came to a door. Once again, he listened. Through the door, he heard a sound that, although muffled, was vaguely familiar. Gun in hand, he flung the door open and stepped inside.

The door opened into a small office that seemed to house nothing but some old filing cabinets, an ancient desk, and a couple of chairs. Mo was seated behind the desk, doing a line of coke. He jumped up, plainly startled, when Kane burst in. An odd grin spread across his face when he saw who had entered.

"Hey, partnah," Mo said, wiping a couple of grains of white powder off his lip with the back of his hand. "Whachu doin' here?"

"Figured we needed to talk," Kane replied.

For the first time, Mo seemed to notice the gun, and the smile slowly vanished. "Everything alright? How'd the pick-up go?"

"You tell me," Kane said, then motioned with the gun for Mo to sit back down while he took a chair on the other side of the desk. "And keep yo hands where I can see 'em."

Taking his seat again, Mo placed his hands flat on the top of the desk. "So, what's this all about?"

"Somebody set me up yesterday when I was supposed to pick up the coke."

"Really?" Mo uttered, looking bug-eyed. "Wasn't me. I got my two hundred kay and you niggas shoulda got the five keys. The only thang I was expectin' after that was to get the rest of my half after you and Jaycee started sellin' that shit."

"So you didn't set me up?"

"I swear, man, no. I didn't do it."

"And I'm s'posed to take yo word for it."

"Look man, you got the gun. I can pretend, but we both know that as long as you got the piece, you got the power, and eventually I'm gonna tell you anything you wanna know."

"So you sayin' that there's no need for this to get messy. You'll just answer my questions without me havin' to use any, uh, extreme methods."

Mo nodded. "Exactly."

"Fine," Kane said. "Where'd the coke come from?"

"Huh?" Mo said. "Whachu mean? It came from my supply line, same as every other key I've ever sold. I just thought I'd try to sommin' diff'rent – goin' straight to the retailer instead of the wholesaler. Thought it would work out better for all parties involved."

Kane snorted in derision. "Now you just said this wouldn't have to get ugly, that you'd answer my questions, and the first thing you do is start lyin'."

"But I'm not, man. I'm tellin' you the truth."

"Okay, that's strike two. Lucky for you, I'm a patient muhfucka, so I'm gonna try one last time: where did the coke come from?"

Mo looked nervous, and Kane could tell that he was thinking, trying to figure out what he could say that would get him out of this situation. Unexpectedly, he seemed to deflate, like all the air went out of him.

"I stole it," Mo confessed.

Kane stared at him for a moment. "Stole what – all five keys?"

Mo nodded. "Yeah."

"From who?"

"One of *my* suppliers."

"Are you crazy?" Kane demanded. "Your suppliers are some of the most violent organizations on the fuckin' planet! Those muhfuckas will slit your throat over fuckin' *grams*, and you steal five *keys*?"

"Yeah, but nobody knows about it," Mo insisted.

"Bullshit," Kane declared flatly. "Five keys can't just disappear and nobody notice. Somebody will miss that shit and coming lookin' for it, and whoever's got it is goin' in a body bag."

"Not this time," Mo countered.

"Okay genius," Kane said. "Explain to me how you pulled this shit off."

"Okay," Mo stated. "Here's how it works…"

Chapter 35

Kane had to admit that what Mo had done was pretty ingenious.

Mo's main business was simply being an operator at the wholesale level; he'd buy off his suppliers and then sell to another wholesaler. He generally never dealt with niggas at the retail level – the dealers who sold on the street.

Occasionally, however, he'd take some work on consignment. If a supplier had some shit he couldn't move for some reason, he might ask Mo to try selling it for him. Under those circumstances, Mo was essentially a salesman working on commission: he'd locate a buyer for the shit and – if everyone agreed on the price – he'd take a cut of the amount paid as his percentage. The higher he could sell for, the bigger his income. It was lucrative, he didn't have to put any cash on the table, and he didn't have to take as many risks as niggas sellin' on the street. But then he got greedy.

Basically, if he got a key of coke on consignment that was, say, ninety-five percent pure, Mo might take five grams out of it. He'd then cut the original batch with something to make up for the missing weight. The end result was that Mo would end up with five grams of coke for himself, and the key he'd taken it from would work out to be something like ninety percent pure instead of ninety-five. (He kept it close enough that the buyer wouldn't complain too much about any discrepancy.)

At first he was doing it just to support his own habit, but quickly realized that it was a way to build up a sellable stash for himself. Over time, taking a few grams at a time, he accumulated five keys. Then, instead of simply selling it at the wholesale level, he got the bright idea to

143

partner up with niggas on the street and shoot for a big payday.

"And here we are," Mo said, after wrapping up his explanation.

"Okay, that explains where you got the five keys," Kane acknowledged. "Still don't tell my why that coke is too hot to touch."

"Well," Mo droned, "there is a teeny, tiny chance that my consignment seller found out that some coke was missing."

"What?!" Kane exclaimed.

However, before Mo could say anything else, the door burst open and four niggas with guns rushed into the room. Kane, leaping to his feet and, after spinning around, realized three things almost at once.

First, he had made the classic error of sitting with his back to the door – not to mention the fact that he'd failed to lock it. Second, he was completely outgunned. Third, he knew these niggas that had come rushing in. As a matter of fact, they worked for him.

"Ray. Jo-Jo. Stank. Bobby," he muttered, rattling off their names. "What da fuck y'all doin' here?"

"You mean, what da fuck they doin' here so *late*," Mo corrected as one of the guys – Bobby – reached out and took Kane's gun. "I had to tell this muhfucka my whole damn life story waitin' on you niggas to show up."

Kane looked at him in surprise. "You knew I was coming."

"I got a heads-up," Mo said with a smile. "Then I just waited by the stairwell door in my garage, peeking out until you pulled in. Didn't want anything crazy happening in my apartment building – can't shit where I eat, ya know – so I led yo ass here. There were a couple of times when

144

I was worried I would lose you, so I ended up driving slow as a muhfucka. But you came through in the end."

"So this was just another set-up, like with the five keys."

"Sorta. But if it's any consolation, I told you the truth about how I got the coke."

"Thanks, that's a relief."

"And just so you know, it's not personal – at least not for *me*. I just need a scapegoat for my consignment supplier regarding the stolen keys."

Kane turned away from him in disgust, looking at the four who had their guns trained on him.

"And you muhfuckas just jumped ship and on his payroll now."

Stank laughed. He was a big bald nigga with rotten teeth and bad breath (which was the source of his nickname).

"Naw, we still on the same payroll," Stank said. "You was just confused in thinkin' that we worked for *you*."

Kane frowned. That was the second time in recent memory that someone he thought was on the payroll mentioned working for someone else. Obviously, he hadn't spent enough time building loyalty to himself in the organization.

Movement from one of the niggas aiming at him got Kane's attention. It was Ray, taking better aim at Kane and seemingly preparing to fire.

"Not here!" Mo belted out. "I don't need to be cleaning up a fuckin' mess in my office. Take his ass somewhere else and do what you need to do."

The quartet stepped away from the door and Ray motioned for Kane to walk back out into the hallway. Kane complied, raising his hands as he left the office.

He walked slowing down the hallway, with the four gunmen close behind him. Arms still raised, he was thinking furiously about how to get out of this when an idea occurred to him.

As he walked down the hallway, he passed a light switch that was positioned a foot or so away from the door that led to the chop-shop area. The minute he was abreast of it, he swiftly dropped his hands, flicking the switch off. As the hallway went dark, Kane dropped low and leaped through the doorway in one fluid motion.

Gunshots immediately rang out in the hallway behind him, and somebody screamed. As he hit the ground and rolled, Kane guessed that one of those fools had shot another, or had gotten clipped by a ricochet or something. However, hearing motion behind him, he didn't have a bunch of time to dwell on it.

Kane had dove through the doorway at an angle. Pulling out Noose's gun – those idiots had failed to search him – he released a couple of shots in the direction of the door to the hallway. He was rewarded with a yelp of pain and the sound of a body hitting the floor, but didn't hang around trying to figure out who he'd hit or if they were down for the count. Staying low, he dashed toward the exit and was outside a second later.

Chapter 36

Mika didn't know what to do.

Kane had only been inside the warehouse for a few minutes when a truck when an extended cab had pulled up, and four niggas had jumped out with guns in their hands. The quartet of new arrivals had immediately dashed inside. She didn't know who they were, but the implications for Kane seemed dire.

Afterwards, she had listened intently but didn't immediately hear anything. (More specifically, she hadn't heard gunfire, which was what she was expecting.) Now she sat there, trying to figure out whether to keep waiting or go in.

On the one hand, she hadn't heard any shots fired. Of course, she didn't know how muffled or distorted the sound would be to someone on the outside, but she was sure she would have picked up on something.

On the other hand, you could do a lot of damage to a nigga without using a gun. Just because nobody had fired a gun, it didn't mean that Kane wasn't in there getting lit up in some other way.

Fuck it, she finally said to herself, and was about to get out when shots rang out.

In truth, if was a short series of muffled booms, and acoustically she honestly couldn't tell where they'd come from, but assumed it was the warehouse. As if in proof of this, Kane came barreling out the door a few seconds later. He ran towards Mo's car, then leaped into the air feet-first and slid across the hood likesome nigga in the movies before dropping to the other side and hunkering down. At the same time, two niggas stuck their heads out the warehouse door – one high and one low – and began firing at him.

Kane's position on the side of Mo's car actually faced Mika's direction, so she had a bird's eye view of everything happening. There was a short exchange of gunfire between Kane and the niggas at the door, and then he just hunkered down. He glanced in her direction, and she could tell by the look on his face that he was judging distance, terrain, speed…

Almost immediately, Mika understood the issue: Kane was out of ammo. The two niggas at the door hadn't figured it out yet, but they would soon as they realized that Kane wasn't returning fire anymore. And being a block away, the SUV was probably too far for him get to without getting gunned down (assuming these niggas were halfway decent shots).

At that point, the two in the door way seemed to figure things out to some degree, because one of them stepped boldly outside. When he didn't get fired on, he appeared to laugh, and a moment later the other nigga stepped out to join him. One of them muttered something, causing the other one to chuckle. Mika couldn't make out what was being said, but they were obviously taunting Kane and making fun of his predicament. A moment later, they began to fan out, with one heading towards the front of Mo's car and the other the rear. That said, they crept forward slowly, plainly aware of the fact that they were possibly being baited.

Mika went into action almost before she was consciously aware of it. Kane had left the SUV's key in the ignition (presumably so she could turn on the heat if she got cold), so she slid into the driver's seat and turned the car on. She then shifted into drive and, with the lights still out, went roaring down the street.

The niggas closing in on Kane were so focused on their quarry that they didn't even notice the vehicle headed in their direction until it was almost on top on them. At that point, Mika had the front passenger-side window rolled down. She hit the brakes just as she went past the back of Mo's car and opened fire.

The two niggas she shot at hadn't even looked in her direction until just before the SUV came to a halt. At that point, with bullets whizzing towards their black asses, they suddenly realized that they were incredibly exposed.

The one near the front of Mo's car dove towards the grill, seeking cover. The other one, realizing that the back of Mo's car offered no advantage (because that's where the bitch with the gun in the SUV was), turned and tried running towards the door, firing blindly behind him. Mika couldn't tell if she hit him or not, but he suddenly went down, practically faceplanting into the concrete.

A gunshot from the front of Mo's car drew her attention, and she suddenly remembered the entire reason she was there: Kane. But she needn't have worried. When she looked, she saw him standing at the front of the vehicle, looking down and holding a gun in a two-handed grip.

Seeing him standing there, she immediately understood what must have happened. Her sudden appearance had taken to the gunmen by surprise, and when the one near the front of the car had sought cover, he'd focused on the immediate threat (Mika) and apparently forgot about the latent one (Kane). Seeing an opportunity, Kane had jumped the nigga, took his gun, and shot him with his own weapon.

Kane seemed to stand there frozen for a moment, then he went into motion. However, instead of heading towards the SUV, he went back into the warehouse.

What da fuck is he doin'? Mika thought, glancing around nervously.

There didn't seem to be anybody in the vicinity and the shots didn't seem to have roused anyone, but she didn't know that for sure. Plus, more niggas could show up any second. They needed to get in the fucking wind.

She heard a shot sound from inside the warehouse, and then two more, although not in immediate succession. A few moments later, Kane walked out the door. The nigga who had faceplanted was still on the ground, moving slowly and moaning. Kane casually shot him in the back of the head as he went by, then dropped the gun on the ground.

Upon reaching the car, he opened the door and climbed into the passenger seat.

"Let's roll," he said calmly.

Mika nodded and drove off.

Chapter 37

They didn't speak initially as Mika drove. Kane had an intense frown on his face, and she sensed that he was deep in thought about something.

"So, what's the plan?" she asked after a few minutes.

Kane let out a groan and muttered, "I'm not sure. There's a lot of shit in play."

Mika simply nodded. Using the controls on her side of the car, she started to raise the passenger side window, which was still down.

"No," Kane ordered. "Leave it down for now."

"What for?" Mika demanded. "It's fuckin' December and freezin' out there."

"You fired a bunch of rounds in here," Kane explained. "Smells like gunsmoke in this bitch, and if it settles into the upholstery it may never come out. Then, every time five-oh pull you over, the car smell like a fuckin' war zone and he got probable cause to search that muhfucka."

"Fine," she relented. "We'll leave it down for now."

"Well, if it's that much of an inconvenience, next time feel free to let 'em cap my ass instead of shootin'," Kane suggested. "Speaking of which…"

He glanced into the rear of the car and then, grunting with effort, began leaning back that way, seemingly feeling around the floor.

Mika watched him for a few seconds (noting that he checked the front of the car as well), then curiosity got the better of her. "Whachu doin'?"

"Shell casings," he replied. "Fingerprints."

151

Of course! Mika could have smacked herself upside the head. Most people load bullets barehanded, meaning their fingers touched the bullet casing. Now she understood why Kane had picked up her shell casings when she'd shot Noose.

"Wait a minute!" she exclaimed. "I thought they weren't able to do that – lift prints from cartridges."

"They ain't perfected the technique yet," Kane said as he straightened up. "But science is improvin' all the time. Might as well start developin' the right habits now."

He groaned again as he put the shell casings in his pocket, causing Mika to look at him in concern.

"You okay?" she asked.

"I'm starting to feel a little sommin'," he said, placing a hand on his stomach where he'd been shot. Gently, he rolled up his shirt, and Mika saw that his bandage wrap was bloodstained. It hadn't soaked through to his shirt, but the bandages definitely needed to be changed.

"Shit!" she exclaimed. "You must have torn your stitches with all that running around. I'm surprised you could stand up straight."

"It's the adrenaline," Kane noted. "It was pumpin' like a muhfucka while those niggas were shootin' at me, and I didn't feel a thang. Now it's starting to wear off."

He opened the glove compartment and reached around inside for a second, then drew out one of the needles Doc had left. Mika knew without asking what was on his agenda.

"I don't think you should be doing that," she remarked. "Doc said one every twenty-four hours, and any more would fuck you up. Countin' the one Doc gave you, that'll be yo third."

"Well, it's either get fucked up by the pain or get fucked up by pain *medicine*," Kane retorted. "I'ma go with the medicine."

Without hesitation (and before Mika could say anything else), he stuck the needle into the area of the wound and pressed down on the plunger. A moment later he withdrew the needle and pulled his shirt back down. He then tossed the needle out the window. Afterwards, he shifted position, seeming to get more comfortable, then closed his eyes. Less than a minute later, he began breathing in and out at a steady measured rate that told Mika he was asleep.

"Told you it would fuck yo ass up, nigga," she muttered, then stealthily rolled the windows back up and cranked the heat up full blast, hoping to get warm for just a second. A minute or two later, no longer feeling that she was going to morph into a black popsicle, she turned her attention back to figuring out where they should be headed. However, she didn't have long to consider the problem, as red-and-blue lights suddenly started flashing behind her.

It was the fucking cops.

Chapter 38

Muthafucka! Mika screamed mentally. They had just been in a gunfight and now this shit. *When it rains, it fuckin' pours...*

The police car quickly pulled behind her, letting her know the SUV was the vehicle of interest (not that there were many other niggas on the road at the moment). Mika began slowing down; at the same time, she reached over and shook Kane.

"Hey, nigga!" she hissed. "Wake yo ass up! The cops are pulling us over!"

Kane slowly opened his eyes and glanced around as Mika came to a stop, looking towards the front of the SUV and then the rear.

"Lights..." he muttered.

Shit! Mika thought. She had never turned the headlights back on!

She quickly turned them on as she glanced in the rearview mirror. The cop was just sitting there (probably running their plates), although he had turned his spotlight on them. That said, Mika was sure he couldn't see the interior of the car. Bearing that in mind, she reached into the back seat and grabbed the bag of coke. Unzipping it, she tossed her gun inside, then nudged Kane, who was starting to doze again.

"Hey!" She whispered fiercely. "Put your piece in the bag!"

She wasn't sure that Kane understood her, but then he pulled out his gun and held it out. Mika took it and dumped it in the bag.

"What about Noose's?" she demanded.

"Left it...at the warehouse," he replied lazily.

Nodding in understanding, Mika quickly zipped the bag closed. Then she hurriedly shoved the bag under her sweatshirt, in the region of her stomach.

"Da fuck you doin'?" muttered Kane, eyes half closed.

"Nigga, I'm carryin' yo muthafuckin' baby," Mika uttered. "That's what I'm fuckin' doin'."

Kane glanced at her stomach. "That's the lumpiest fuckin' kid I ever seen." He then closed his eyes and seemed to fall asleep.

"PLEASE LOWER ALL YOUR WINDOWS," a voiced suddenly boomed from a loudspeaker. Needless to say, it was the cop.

Mika did as she was told, letting all the windows down, hoping in the back of her mind that any smell of gunsmoke was now gone. There was a bit of a cold wind blowing, and she mentally crossed her fingers and prayed that it would enough to make it difficult to catch the scent of anything.

Despite the glare from the spotlight, she saw in the rearview and side mirrors that there were actually *two* cops, with one approaching on each side of the vehicle. For a second, she fought panic as her mind flipped back to the gunfight. Had any of those niggas managed to hit the passenger side of the car? Mika didn't think so, but if they had it was too late to do anything about it now. Still, she watched the cop on the passenger side closely, waiting to see if anything seemed to draw his attention.

Fortunately, the cop in question didn't seem to care too much about the external condition of the SUV. He was more focused on the interior, shining his flashlight inside and scoping it out, as did his partner on the driver's side. As far as Mika knew, there was nothing back there – not in the rear seat area, anyway, but she personally had never checked the cargo space. She just assumed that it was clear.

As the cops reached the front doors of the vehicle, Mika placed her left hand protectively over her belly, keeping her right on the wheel. Suddenly, there was a light in her face.

"Morning ma'am," said the cop at her door – a white guy in his mid-forties who was kind enough to take the light out of her face after a second.

"Good morning, officer," Mika said with a smile in her sweetest, least-combative voice. Looking at his nameplate, she noticed it gave his last name as Dobson

"Do you know why we pulled you over?" Dobson asked.

"Probably the headlights," she said, gesturing towards the front of the car. "I forgot to turn them on and only realized it when you pulled behind me."

"Where you headed to this early?"

"We're coming from the hospital," she replied. "We had a scare last night with the baby." As she spoke, she rubbed her stomach. "I started feeling some discomfort and my husband" – she glanced at Kane – "sort of went into panic mode. It's our first, and he's always terrified something's going to happen."

The cop on the passenger side shined his light in Kane's face, who moaned slightly and turned away from the light.

"What's wrong with him?" asked the second cop.

"Nothing," Mika assured him. "It turned out the only thing wrong with me was…was gas." She looked down momentarily, as if embarrassed, still rubbing her stomach. "Anyway, just to be safe, they kept me for observation for about six hours. Just lying in bed, I was able to get some sleep, but apparently my husband stayed up the whole time, worried sick. When they finally released me, he was worn out, so one of the doctors gave him something to help him sleep."

"Hmmm," droned the cop on Kane's side, obviously not fully convinced by Mika's story.

"You got your license on you?" asked Dobson.

Mika shook her head. "No. We left in such a hurry that I didn't grab anything – not even my purse."

"What about *him*?" asked the officer, nodding at Kane.

Mika, trying to keep her face passive, leaned over and shook Kane.

"Honey," she said. "Honey. These officers need to see your license."

Kane seemed to struggle to wake up. "Huh?"

"Baby, the police need to see your driver's license," Mika repeated.

Kane looked at Dobson for a moment, and then at his partner. Both officer's hand their free hands resting on the butts of their service revolvers.

Kane slowly raised both hands in the air.

"Wallet," he muttered, pointing down with his right index finger towards his rear right pocket.

Keeping his left hand in the air, Kane slowly reached towards the pocket in question with his right, at the same time leaning forward. A few seconds later, after jiggling his hand side to side a little bit, he slowly lifted it, revealing a black wallet. Next he flipped it open and took out what appeared to be a license, which he handed to the officer outside his window.

The officer shined his light on it, then back on Kane's face. Turning his attention back to the license, he seemed to inspect it intently for a few moments.

"This is out-of-state," the officer finally said.

"Sorry – just moved here," Kane explained. "Haven't had a chance to get an in-state one yet."

The cop appeared to contemplate this for a moment, then seemed to have a silent exchange with his partner over the roof of the SUV.

"Do you need to see the registration?" Kane asked, pointing at the glove compartment.

"Uh, that's not necessary," Dobson replied. Looking at Mika, he said, "We're going to let you go, but please keep your headlights on, ma'am."

"I will, officer, from now on," she assured him.

"And try to get a state license as soon as possible," Dobson's partner suggested, handing the license back to Kane.

"Yes, sir," Kane said. "Soon as I can."

The officers turned and began walking back to their vehicle, and Mika had to fight the desire to peel rubber getting away from there.

Chapter 39

After the incident with the cops, it felt like five minutes before Mika could breathe again. Honestly, she couldn't believe that pregnancy shit had worked.

She looked at Kane; he appeared slightly groggy, but hadn't gone back to sleep.

"Good thinking with those cops," he stated in a voice that was almost a whisper. "Keep it up, and I'll make you my ride-or-die bitch."

"Thanks," she said, smiling softly. "So what was that with the out-of-state license shit?"

"It's fake, but looks like it's from a state that doesn't share driver's license info. That being the case, cops know it's a waste of their time to run it."

"That's smart," Mika acknowledged.

"Yeah, well, you gotta think ahead if you wanna stay alive in this game," he said.

"Well, you obviously too fucked up at the moment to do much of anything," she said.

"We just need to find a place for me to rest for a hot minute," he argued, closing his eyes. "Then I'll be good as new."

"So what – you wanna go back out to yo place in the country?"

Kane shrugged. "Prolly. I got a spot in the city, but Jaycee know 'bout it."

Mika knew what was being implied, even if her passenger didn't say the words. "So, yo homey Jaycee is the one who set you up?"

Kane didn't immediately answer. "Let's just find a spot first. Some place that'll gimme a minute to think about this shit."

SHE'S HIS DRUG, HE'S HER THUG

"I think I know a place – and not all the way in Bumfuck, Egypt neither."

"Whatever," Kane mumbled. "Just get me there."

Chapter 40

The apartment seemed larger than Mika remembered. In truth, it was still a fuckin' rinky-dink efficiency about the size of a breadbox, but after living on the road and out of bags for five months, it seemed like a damned palace.

Fortunately, it was still early when they arrived, and she and Kane had been able to get inside without being seen (although she'd had to half-carry him, much like the day before). The place was generally clean, so her brother hadn't lied about keeping the apartment tidy, but it looked like the same sheets were on the bed that were on it when she left. Not knowing what the fuck her brother's "tenants" had been up to, she had Kane rest on a sofa in the living room area while she changed them.

There was some clean linen in the closet, and in no time at all she had the bed ready. However, before she let him lie down, she took him into the bathroom. Once there, she cleaned and dressed his wound the way Doc had instructed her. Kane was practically dead on his feet by the time she guided him to the bed and had him lay down. He fell asleep immediately.

Finally having a break for the first time in hours, Mika stretched out next to him. In no time at all, she was asleep as well.

****

Mika woke to a sensation that was both familiar and pleasurable: someone kissing her neck while fondling her tits under the sweatshirt she still wore. At the same time, she felt something hard and solid pressing up against her ass. She smiled and opened her eyes for a moment, remembering exactly where she was this time (as well as who was spooning her).

Moaning gently with desire, she reached behind her, toward Kane's groin, and was rewarded with a rock-hard dick almost springing into her palm. He groaned as she stroked his shaft, ran her fingers lightly over his balls.

He placed a hand on her shoulder and tugged gently, indicating he wanted her to lie on her back. She complied, and he shifted position, getting on top her without putting his full weight on her. Still playing with her tits, He kissed his way up her neck, to her chin...

"Uh-uh," she muttered as he was about to kiss her lips, putting her hand to his mouth and pushing gently while turning her face away.

Kane froze. "You want me to stop?"

"Only trying to kiss me," she said. "I haven't brushed my teeth."

"Oh, that's cool," he muttered. "Long as we can still fuck."

Mika laughed. "You know, you one smooth-talking, nigga – really know how to sweep a bitch off her feet with that poetry you be spoutin'."

"So, is that a yes?" Kane asked. "'Cause these days a nigga gotta get full authorization – get papers notarized and shit – before he even think about tapping some ass."

"Yeah, nigga, it's a yes," Mika said, smiling. "We can still fuck. We may just have to improvise"

As she spoke, she lightly nudged him, indicating that he should move off her, and he complied. Drawing up her knees, she swiftly slid her panties and sweats off, then rolled onto her stomach.

Chapter 41

They fucked doggy-style that time, with Mika on her hands and knees on the bed and Kane ramming her from behind. It had taken a moment to coordinate their movements, to get the rhythm down, but once they did that shit felt fantastic.

Both of them came explosively, at the same time. Kane in particular left nothing on the table, damn near matching the volume of Mika's screams with his groans before practically collapsing on top of her as he breathed heavily in and out, hands gently squeezing her tits.

To Mika, the sense of bliss she'd felt before returned, but in a way that was more expansive. In that moment, with a man on her, behind her and in her – all at the same time – she felt a certain sense of completeness. It was as if she were enveloped by warmth and happiness, but understood that it was something that went beyond mere sex. And as he slid out of her, methodically and lovingly kissing her back as he did so, she knew that Kane felt the same.

He collapsed onto his back, while Mika lowered herself onto the bed and then rolled into his arms. They lay like that for a few minutes, neither of them saying anything.

"So what now?" Mika finally asked.

Kane sighed. "I gotta handle up on Jaycee."

"Are you positive he set you up?"

"Mo practically admitted it. Plus somebody gave him a heads-up that I'd be headed his way, and those niggas that tried to take me out actually work for us."

"Seems pretty cut-and-dry."

"More than that," Kane stated, "when I went back into the warehouse after the gunfight, it wasn't just to take care of that fool Mo. I needed to get my piece back as well, but mostly I wanted Mo's cell to see who he'd been talking to."

He paused, prompting Mika to ask, "And?"

Kane let out a sigh. "He got a call from Jaycee – right after we left him and Jade."

Chapter 42

Kane got dressed and went out a short time later, intent on picking up a couple of toothbrushes, as well as something to eat (not to mention dumping all the shell casings he had collected). It wasn't until he'd been gone about five minutes that Mika realized it was possible that the nigga wouldn't come back.

Wouldn't that be a fuckin' movie cliché? she thought. *Fuck some dumb bitch's brains out, then run off with the car, the drugs and the money while her ass is still over the muthafuckin' rainbow thinkin' about the smooth dickin' she just got.*

She hated to do it (because it evidenced a lack of faith in Kane), but she did a quick check of her shit. Thankfully, nothing was missing – not her wallet, not her gun, not the bankroll from her brother. That said, the bag with the five keys *was* gone. So maybe the nigga had run off, but just decided to be halfway decent about it.

She was still weighing the matter in her mind when a knock sounded at the door and she recognized Kane softly saying, "It's me."

****

It had been mid-morning when they had fucked, having gotten only a couple of hours of sleep. Thus, when Kane had gone out, there had actually been a few places open, despite the fact that it was Sunday. Thus, he'd managed to round up pancakes, eggs and sausages from a fast food place, and scooped up some hygiene and grooming items (including toothbrushes) from a service station.

165

After quickly brushing their teeth, they began to eat before the food got cold, sitting at a small breakfast table.

They had only taken a few bites when Kane, grinning, asked, "So were you surprised?"

Mika frowned. "About what?"

"That I came back. You had this look of relief on yo face when you opened the door and saw me there, like 'Oh, thank heaven – he's returned.'" He said the last part in a sing-song, white-girl kind of voice, and then started chuckling.

Mika just stared at him for a moment, and then said, "Ya know what? Yeah, I *was* surprised to see yo ass. Most niggas, you give'em a piece of pussy and you never have to worry about seeing they sorry-ass again. With you, I done tried three times and still can't get ridda yo ass."

At this point, Kane was cracking up, and a few seconds later, Mika joined him.

When he could finally speak again, he said, "I wish you'd been this funny when we were fuckin'. Then I woulda got sommin' out of it."

Mika's mouth dropped open in faux surprise. Picking up some eggs with her fork, she flicked them at him, then burst out laughing as they spattered on his face. As he wiped them off – grinning to show he was a good sport – she flicked more at him. His grin wasn't quite as broad as he cleaned eggs off his face a second time, which almost sent her into a giggling fit. She was getting ready to go for it a third time when he suddenly leaned over and grabbed her wrist.

His grip was firm but not painful, and the look on his face showed that he was being playful. Giving her a solid yank, he pulled her around the table towards him, and the next thing she knew she was sitting in his lap.

Mika jerked her arm wildly for a few seconds, grunting with effort as she tried to get free of his grip. He held her just long enough for her to understand that she couldn't get away, then released her.

For a moment, she just sat there, looking into his eyes. There was an intimacy in that stare, something shared that she hadn't really felt with any other man.

Unexpectedly, she shifted her position, swinging her leg over so that she was straddling him. Taking his face in her hands while he placed his on her waist, she leaned down and kissed him, longingly and passionately.

On his part, Kane returned the kiss eagerly. He didn't know what it was, but this girl had fascinated him from the moment he'd seen her in that closet. Since bumping into her again, everything in his life had been going at fucking light speed, including their relationship (assuming you could call it that). In less than a day, she had his ass not just pussy-whipped, but damn near mesmerized.

Of course, he'd never admit that out loud, but at this point, he didn't have to; his fucking body announced it every time he looked at her: his eyes always finding their way to her tits and curves (even when she was in sweats). His dick getting hard enough to drive nails every time he thought about hitting that ass. His mouth starting to water just dreaming about eating that pussy... In all honesty, he hadn't felt this way about a female in a long time – maybe never.

Like most niggas, he had practically fallen in love with the first girl to give him a piece of tail, had thought she was an angel just because she spread her legs for him. In truth, she'd been a fuckin' bitch who didn't care about anybody but herself and would let any nigga who bought her a two-piece chicken box stick dick to her.

SHE'S HIS DRUG, HE'S HER THUG

In a similar vein, the first girl to give him a decent blowjob had also blown his mind. She'd been a "good" girl – hadn't wanted to give up the ass, but would go down on you in a minute. He'd been so strung out behind her that he'd honestly thought he could go through life without pussy, as long as those spectacular blowjobs continued.

Mika, however, was altogether different. With her, you expected the fucking to be good because of that bod she had, but in truth the sex (including the oral) was on another level entirely. It was so intense, so engrossing, that it defied explanation. And on top of that, the chick had a brain, as evidenced by how she'd dealt with the cops earlier. In short, she had a killer bod, and the mind to go with it. Kane knew that if he wasn't careful, he could fall hard for this bitch – if he hadn't already…

Chapter 43

The rest of breakfast consisted mostly of Mika sitting in Kane's lap and feeding him. It wasn't anything she had planned; she hadn't even known she was going to do it. However, after their kiss ended, she had reached around, grabbed his plate and fork, and started putting food in his mouth.

Mika actually enjoyed it. She'd known women who felt subservient doing this kind of stuff (and maybe it did feel that way with certain guys) but that was far from the case at the moment. There was an intimacy to the act of feeding a man like this – a closeness and affinity that sprang from a powerful, burgeoning connection.

After she was done feeding Kane (which only took a few minutes), Mika moved back to her original seat to finish her own breakfast. Much to her surprise, Kane spent that time cleaning up the eggs she had thrown at him. She smiled watching him wipe scrambled eggs off the table and floor, thinking how nice it was to come across a man who didn't think domestic labor was demeaning or "woman's work."

Following breakfast, she had dragged him to the bathroom and into the shower with her. He'd been reluctant at first – after all, it was a tub and shower combo in an efficiency (translation: tiny as fuck) – but once they were in and the water turned on, he surprised her yet again.

Taking the soap and towel from her, Kane lovingly bathed her from head to toe. For Mika, having him lather her all over, spreading the soap over almost every square inch of her skin with his hands, was incredibly arousing. Likewise when he took the towel and used it to scrub her clean (especially when he took it between her legs).

SHE'S HIS DRUG, HE'S HER THUG

There was no sex this time, however. Just a sensual and exciting series of touches and caresses. It was almost like a game, and was repeated when she turned the tables and bathed him. Of course, his bandages were a concern – they weren't supposed to get wet – but the same thought apparently occurred to both of them: bandages could be replaced, so there was no need to let them interfere with the sensuous play they were involved in.

It wasn't until they got out of the shower and were drying off that Mika suddenly realized something: they hadn't spoken in quite a while. All of the communication between them since breakfast had been in the form of looks and gestures, touch and feel. It struck her as a little weird, but at the same time felt...right.

She was still dwelling on the subject when Kane's voice cut into her thoughts.

"So," he began as he dried himself, "why didn't *you* leave?"

Mika gave him a confused look. "Huh?"

"You've had a coupla opportunities to take off with the keys. Even at wholesale prices, you coulda offloaded them and picked up a nice piece of change – enough to start over somewhere."

"I ain't never liked the drug game. It was never the kind of shit I wanted to get caught up in, 'cause I never heard of anybody doin' that shit and then retirin' to the beach. Yo ass always end up dead, in jail, or in a wheelchair."

"So I guess you ain't interested in a nigga who been livin' that lifestyle."

"Depends on what's more important to him: being a drug-dealin' thug or bein' with me."

170

Kane merely nodded, seeming to ponder what she'd said.

Afterwards, they hurriedly got dressed, with Mika changing Kane's bandages once again.

"So what now?" she asked as she finished wrapping gauze around him.

Kane sighed. "Now I go handle shit with Jaycee."

Mika looked Kane in the eye and boldly asked, "Are you gonna kill 'im?"

"I dunno," Kane admitted. "Could you kill yo sister, even if she fucked you over like that? Set you up? Sent niggas to take you out?"

Mika shrugged. "I dunno."

"Then you know how I feel. I mean, Jaycee's my boy. We been in the fuckin' trenches together, with him havin' my back when nobody else did, and me havin' his. I just can't believe he'd be this foul – not with *me*."

"Money changes people," Mika reminded him.

"But not *us*. Me and Jaycee were solid through thick and thin together, and with this deal we were finally gonna blow up."

"Or maybe the plan was for one of you to blow up," Mika shot back. "And for the other to get *lit* up."

Kane just looked at her for a moment, then lowered his head. "Guess there's only one way to find out."

"Alright then. Let's go."

Kane looked at her in concern. "Fuck naw. You staying' here. If Jaycee willin' to set me up, he damn sho won't care by blasting a hole in *you*."

"Fuck that!" Mika retorted. "We in this shit together now, nigga, so you ain't leavin' me behind. And don't forget how many times I saved yo black ass just in the last day."

Kane looked like he wanted to argue some more, but one glance at Mika's face told him that this was one fight he wasn't going to win.

"Alright," he finally said. "Let's go get this shit sorted."

Chapter 44

Kane and Mika were already inside and waiting in the apartment above the bar when Jaycee and Jade came in from church. To be honest, however, it had been brunch *after* church that they were returning from, and they were stunned to see someone in their place.

Jade had entered first, strutting in like a celebrity, with shades on her face and a designer bag on her arm. However, she actually froze as she stepped inside and saw Kane sitting on the couch in their living room, holding his own gun as well as Jaycee's shotgun. Jaycee, entering behind her, didn't really notice anything at first.

'Why you standin' here like a muhfuckin' statue?" he asked Jade, who removed her shades and simply stared at Kane. "What da hell is wrong with…"

Jaycee trailed off as he saw Kane sitting there with two guns trained on him and his girl. Unexpectedly, the door slammed closed behind him, and Jaycee turned to find Mika there, also holding a gun on them.

"Kane," Jaycee said, "what da fuck is goin' on here?"

"That's what I wanna know," Kane replied. "Come on over so we can talk about it."

He motioned with the shotgun, at which point Jaycee and Jade did as instructed, walking into the living room and taking a seat on a loveseat directly across from Kane, who was joined on the couch by Mika. Without being told, Jaycee kept his hands where they could plainly be seen. There was a coffee table in between the couch and loveseat the two couples were respectively sitting on, but an agile nigga could clear that in one easy leap. However, since Kane had both weapons trained on his friend, Jaycee was unlikely to try anything like that.

"So, where'd you go eat?" Kane asked casually.

Jaycee cleared his throat. "A little spot downtown that serves a champagne brunch on Sundays."

Kane looked at Mika. "See, I told you: Jaycee's a creature of habit. Church every Sunday, and then going to get something to eat." He turned his attention back to Jaycee. "I told you a million times, nigga: you gotta vary yo routine, or you gonna make it easy for muhfuckas to set up on you."

"That what this is?" asked Jaycee. "A set-up?"

Kane shook his head. "Naw, the set-up was yesterday. And early this mornin'. Prolly another one later today if I don't get shit handled."

"We ain't have shit to do with that, so get the fuck out my house," Jade interjected, looking furious. "How you even get in here anyway?"

Kane laughed. "Well, Ms. Thang, before this was yo house, this is where yo boyfriend and I conducted business, and I took charge of minimizing any risks associated with our trade. In other words, I'm the muhfucka who set up security for this bitch. I'm the one who oversaw installation of the alarm system. I'm the one who established the safety protocols. I'm the nigga who came up with the passwords."

"So fuckin' what?" Jade asked.

"Well, after he hooked up with yo ass, Jaycee decided to pimp this bitch out and live here. But knowing him like I do, I knew he wouldn't switch any of the security shit."

Jade gave her boyfriend an evil look, then began slapping at him, saying, "You stupid, dumb-ass, muhfuckin' nigga!"

"Hey! Hey! Hey!" Jaycee shouted, grabbing her wrists. "Changin' them damn codes would'na kept him out anyway!"

"Huh?" Jade muttered, calming down enough so that Jaycee let her go. "What da fuck does that mean?"

"I think Jaycee is talkin' 'bout the history of this building," Kane explained. "See, this buildin' is 'bout a hundred years old, and back during Prohibition, it was a speakeasy. You know 'bout Prohibition, don'chu?"

"Yeah, muhfucka," Jade hissed. "It's when it was against the law to get drunk."

"Sommin' like that," Kane acknowledged. "Anyway, speakeasies like this bar were places where people could slip in and drink alcohol. Now they got raided lotsa times, but most speakeasies had secret passageways for VIPs to get out if the cops showed up. This place has one, and me and Jaycee decided to keep it in case five-oh ever broke the door down, although we the only ones that knew about it or had the key."

"Yeah," Jaycee said. "But I never thought my boy would use it to get the drop on me."

"You keep overlooking the fact that I'm the one who got set up," Kane stated, then winced. "I forgot to mention that I also got shot."

"And I keep tellin' you, man, that wasn't *me*," Jaycee insisted.

"Then why is it that the second I leave here, tellin' you I'm goin' to see Mo, he gets a call from you?" Kane asked. "Next thing I know, niggas that s'posed to work for us – *us*, muhfucka – rollin' up tryin' to put one in my dome."

"No fuckin' way, nigga," Jaycee insisted, looking angry. "I ain't call Mo, and I ain't sent nobody after yo ass."

"That's funny," Kane said with a nod. "'Cause that nigga Mo's phone got a call from you on it right around the time we left."

"Bullshit!" Jaycee shouted.

"Naw, nigga," Kane shot back. "It ain't bullshit at all. Yo name pop right up."

"Nigga, you stupid or something?" Jaycee spat out. "You can put any name you want on a number. I can program a number in my cell and name the caller as fuckin' Martin Luther King if I want to – don't mean a muhfucka gonna be callin' me up shouting 'I have a dream.'"

"Alright," Kane muttered. "I know how to end this shit."

He seemed to contemplate for a moment, then laid the shotgun down lengthwise on the edge of the coffee table in front of him. Keeping his gun pointed at the couple on the loveseat, Kane groaned audibly as he reached into an interior coat pocket with his free hand and pulled out Mo's cell.

"You claim this wasn't you who called Mo and tipped him off," Kane said, "so let's just see. I'm dialin' this muhfucka now, so you bettah pray I go deaf, 'cause if I hear a phone ring in here, this shit's gettin' real."

As he spoke, Kane pressed the call-back button on Mo's cell and then turned on the speakerphone. The tension in the room was almost tangible as the cell searched for a signal for a moment, and then found one. A second later, they could all hear a ringing through Mo's receiver.

Listening intently, no one heard a phone ringing anywhere in the apartment. Jaycee seemed to breathe a sigh of relief, and the tension in the air began to ease, even as the sound of ringing came from Mo's phone a second time.

This time, however, there was a reciprocal ring, coming from somewhere in the apartment. Close by, in fact – and coming from where Jaycee and Jade were sitting.

Suddenly alarmed, Kane began raising his gun towards Jaycee, then winced in pain and grabbed his side.

"Kane!" Mika shouted, turning her attention to him.

At that moment, faster than seemed possible, Jade lunged across the coffee table and grabbed the shotgun, pumping it as she came back to her feet.

"Stay back, muhfuckas!" she ordered as she began slowly backing away, covering the others with the shotgun, including Jaycee. "And drop the fuckin' guns!"

Kane and Mika, still on the couch, set their pieces on the floor.

"Baby," Jaycee said, coming to his feet. "Whachu doin'?"

"Nigga, what it look like I'm doin'?" she demanded.

"The ringing," Mika noted. "It's comin' from her purse."

"Turn that muhfuckin' phone off!" Jade demanded.

Kane stopped the call on Mo's phone, and the ringin' stopped.

"So, it was you," Kane surmised. "You the one that set me up – at the pick-up and at that warehouse with Mo. Your calls and texts all show up as coming from Jaycee, 'cause your cell's in his name. It's one of the clean phones he uses for anything legit."

"This shit was supposed to be simple," Jade muttered. Looking at Kane, she blurted out, "Yo ass was s'posed to die. Why the fuck couldn't you just catch a bullet and go into the dirt like any other nigga?"

"But why, baby?" asked Jaycee. "Didn't we have everything? Didn't I *give* you everything?"

"Can't you see, nigga? Jade asked him. "I'm doin' all this shit for *you*!"

"For *me*?" Jaycee blurted out, looking nonplussed. "Settin' up Kane – my partnah, my brutha – was for *me*?"

"Yes, fool!" Jade exclaimed. "Only one muhfucka can run the show! Ain't no co-kings in this shit. One ruler, one law. Yo ass ain't see it, but Kane was takin' over."

"Bullshit!" Kane spat out. "I ain't never tried to push Jaycee out."

"You didn't have to *try*," Jade explained. "That shit was happenin' on it's own. Everybody always sayin' you the brains of this fuckin' crew. If Jaycee give a muhfucka an order they don't like, niggas be talkin' 'bout, 'Well, what Kane say about it.' All these niggas respectin' you more than Jaycee. It was just a matter of time before he was nothing but yo fuckin' lieutenant."

"So you waited until we got a shot to blow up and and then made yo move," Kane stated.

"Muhfucka, I'm the only reason y'all niggas got a shot in the first place," Jade retorted. "Who you thank convinced Mo to hook up with you niggas? I had to break him off a piece of pussy to do it, but he agreed."

"Da fuck?!" Jaycee exclaimed, looking at Jade like he'd never seen her before. "You fucked Mo?!"

"Nigga, get off yo fuckin' high horse," Jade sneered. "You been taggin' these nasty-ass hoes left and right, and you wonder why I make yo ass wear a rubber. Plus, all they do is get you to buy shit for 'em. At least when I fuck somebody else, it's for *us* to get sommin' out of it."

Jaycee just shook his head in disbelief, like he couldn't come to grips with what he was hearing.

"What about Noose?" asked Kane. "I know you didn't fuck him since you ain't his type."

"Ha!" Jade barked. "No, ain't no dick swinging below *this* waist. Nothin' between these legs but a slice of heaven that most muhfuckas will strangle they momma for. But if you must know, I recruited half the niggas in y'all crew. They loyal to *me*, muhfucka! They work for *me*!"

Kane nodded. "Now it all makes sense. All these fools that joined up with us since we started expandin'… Jaycee told me he vetted them, but he didn't. They all came through *you*. He brought 'em on because you suggested 'em and he trusted you."

"Why wouldn't he trust me?" Jade asked. "He tells me everything, and I keep all his secrets. But I could tell from jump that if he was gonna run the streets one day, we needed to get ridda *you*. And I was gonna need niggas who were loyal to *me* to get it done."

"Well, yo lil' personal army is down by five," Mika interjected.

"Bitch, ain't nobody ask you nuthin'." Jade said to her. "And I can get more niggas at the drop of a hat. Matter of fact, I already had my peeps go by and clean up that mess y'all left at Mo's warehouse, although all they really did was just drag those two bodies inside."

"*Yo* peeps?" Jaycee muttered, finally finding his voice again.

"Yeah, nigga," Jade answered. "Ain't you been listenin'?"

"So what now?" Kane asked.

Jade gave him a sad look. "And all this time I been sayin' *you* the smart one."

"You gone kill us," Mika surmised.

"At least somebody round this bitch is keeping score," Jade declared. "Now, how we finish this thing can go fast or slow, but trust me, gettin' body parts blasted off one at a time with a shotgun ain't nobody's idea of a spa day."

"You want the five keys," Kane said.

"Dammit, I gotta revise my opinion again," Jade admitted. "You *are* smart."

"So why didn't you just have Noose take me out after we got the coke?" Kane asked. "He woulda had the opportunity and you coulda avoided all this."

"Because that brainless shithead woulda found a way to fuck it up, so I knew I needed other hitters," Jade stated. "But that's enough with the chitchat. Let's get down to business."

"Okay, I'll hand the keys over, no fuss," Kane assured her. "But you have to let Mika go."

"Nigga, I ain't gotta do shit," Jade announced. "You cough up the keys, and maybe, just maybe, I'll let this ghetto ho walk outta here on her own two feet."

"Good enough," Kane said. "The coke is in an SUV parked about a block away. But look, that coke is fuckin' radioactive – it's gonna get you killed."

"You talkin' 'bout the folks Mo stole it from?" Jade inquired. "We just need someone to point the figure at. Those fools don't even know how much was stolen from them. So long as they get to make an example outta somebody, they'll be happy."

"And that'll be us," Mika concluded.

"Nothing personal," Jade said to her. "Anyway, it's been nice chattin' with you, but I got shit to take care of."

With that, she raised the shotgun.

"No!" Jaycee belted out, finally finding his tongue again. He quickly stepped over the coffee table, placing himself between Jade and her intended targets.

"Babe," Jade called out, "you might wanna step aside."

"No – fuck that," Jaycee insisted. "You're not doin' this."

"Jaycee, I really like you," Jade stated. "You look nice, treat me decent, and know how to slang that dick when a bitch is in heat. But I'm too close to let you get in my way, and if you don't think I got the balls to run these streets, you got another thing comin'. So come over here and join yo queen, or go into a hole with these two."

Jaycee seemed to hesitate for a second, unclear on what he wanted to do.

"Go on, bruh," Kane said to him. "Step aside and let her finish this shit."

"Naw, man," Jaycee stated, finding his resolve. "All the shit we been through together, lookin' out for each other, bein' there for each other... It wasn't all so I could run out on you at the last minute."

Jaycee turned back to Jade. "Do what you gotta do."

Jade shrugged. "It's yo funeral, nigga."

Then she pulled the trigger.

Chapter 45

The shotgun blast blew Jade about ten feet backwards; she landed hard on the floor, rolling over a couple of times before coming to rest on her back.

"No!" Jaycee wailed, and a moment later he was racing towards her, with Mika and Kane right behind him.

When they reached her, Mika put a hand up to her mouth. Jade was still alive – barely – but it was clear that there was nothing they could do for her. Her torso was shredded, and blood was flowing freely from her mouth.

Crying openly, Jaycee dropped to his knees and took her head in his lap.

"Why, baby," he moaned. "Why?"

Jade didn't seem to hear him. In fact, it was as if she didn't even notice him. Instead, her eyes were focused solely on Kane.

"Like…I…said…" she wheezed between bloody lips. "Smart…"

Kane didn't say anything but knew what she was getting at. Jade then looked up at Jaycee and smiled – and then her head lolled lifelessly to the side.

Kane didn't know what to say. Instead, he just gave Jaycee a firm, supportive pat on the shoulder.

"The shotgun," Jaycee said flatly.

Kane nodded. "Yeah."

Basically, Kane and Mika had used the hidden passage to gain entry to Jaycee and Jade's place. Once inside, Kane had gotten Jaycee's shotgun and rigged it to backfire. The rest – putting the weapon within reach of Jaycee and Jade, Kane's wound allegedly bothering him, etcetera – had all been an act.

182

"In all honesty," Kane said, "I really did think it was you, man. But after everything we been through together, I didn't think I could shoot you."

"So you arranged it so I'd shoot myself," Jaycee concluded.

"Only if you tried to gun me down."

Jaycee nodded. "So what now?"

"For me, nuthin'," Kane said. "I'm done with this shit – this life, man."

Jaycee snorted derisively. "You can thank that, but *this* life, this thuggish hood life we live…that bitch never let you go."

"I gotta try," Kane said, glancing at Mika. "Anyway, I left the five keys in yo bedroom."

Jaycee gave him an odd look. "You don't want 'em? Not even yo share?"

"Naw, man – like I said, I'm getting outta the life," Kane reminded him. "But b'foe you put those keys on the street, you prolly need to clean house – make sure yo crew is really *yo* crew."

With that, he took Mika's hand and – after retrieving their guns – they left.

****

They made it back to the car without incident. As Kane started the engine, Mika gave him an odd look.

"I can't believe you gave up those five keys," she stated in wonder.

Kane pondered for a moment, then asked, "You think it was a mistake? That I should have kept 'em – or at least my half?"

183

Mika shook her head. "No, I'm just surprised. Most niggas wouldn't just walk away from a drug score worth two mill."

"I don't need that score anymore," he explained. "*You* my drug now."

With that, he leaned over and kissed her in a deep and needful way that made her head spin.

After a few moments, he broke away, again saying, "You my drug…and I'm completely addicted."

Fighting a smile, Mika blurted out, "Nigga, just drive the car with yo thuggish ass."

With a grin starting to form on her face, she reached over and took his hand, getting a smile from him in return as they drove away.

THE END

*Mika and Kane will return in *She's His Drug, He's Her Thug 2*.

Thank you for purchasing this book! If you enjoyed it, please feel free to leave a review on the site from which it was purchased.

Also, if you would like to be notified when I release new books, please subscribe to my mailing list via the following link: http://eepurl.com/gShzML

Finally, for those who may be interested, I have included my blog and social media info:

Blog: https://nirvanablaque.blogspot.com/

Facebook: https://www.facebook.com/nirvana.black.3597

Twitter: https://twitter.com/BlaqueNirvana

Made in United States
Orlando, FL
08 September 2022

22203702R00104